PRAISE FOR THE DEA

Here are some of the over 100,000 five star reviews left for the Dead Cold Mystery series.

"Rex Stout and Michael Connelly have spawned a protege."

AMAZON REVIEW

"So begins one damned fine read."

AMAZON REVIEW

"Mystery that's more brain than brawn."

AMAZON REVIEW

"I read so many of this genre...and ever so often I strike gold!"

AMAZON REVIEW

"This book is filled with action, intrigue, espionage, and everything else lovers of a good thriller want."

AMAZON REVIEW

BLOOD INTO WINE
A DEAD COLD MYSTERY

BLAKE BANNER

RIGHTHOUSE

Copyright © 2024 by Right House

All rights reserved.

The characters and events portrayed in this ebook are fictitious. Any similarity to real persons, living or dead, is coincidental and not intended by the author.

No part of this book may be reproduced in any form or by any electronic or mechanical means, including information storage and retrieval systems, without written permission from the author, except for the use of brief quotations in a book review.

ISBN-13: 978-1-63696-015-9

ISBN-10: 1-63696-015-4

Cover design by: Damonza

Printed in the United States of America

www.righthouse.com

www.instagram.com/righthousebooks

www.facebook.com/righthousebooks

twitter.com/righthousebooks

DEAD COLD MYSTERY SERIES
An Ace and a Pair (Book 1)
Two Bare Arms (Book 2)
Garden of the Damned (Book 3)
Let Us Prey (Book 4)
The Sins of the Father (Book 5)
Strange and Sinister Path (Book 6)
The Heart to Kill (Book 7)
Unnatural Murder (Book 8)
Fire from Heaven (Book 9)
To Kill Upon A Kiss (Book 10)
Murder Most Scottish (Book 11)
The Butcher of Whitechapel (Book 12)
Little Dead Riding Hood (Book 13)
Trick or Treat (Book 14)
Blood Into Wine (Book 15)
Jack In The Box (Book 16)
The Fall Moon (Book 17)
Blood In Babylon (Book 18)
Death In Dexter (Book 19)
Mustang Sally (Book 20)
A Christmas Killing (Book 21)
Mommy's Little Killer (Book 22)
Bleed Out (Book 23)

Dead and Buried (Book 24)
In Hot Blood (Book 25)
Fallen Angels (Book 26)
Knife Edge (Book 27)
Along Came A Spider (Book 28)
Cold Blood (Book 29)
Curtain Call (Book 30)

ONE

Deputy Inspector John Newman entered the detectives' room on hesitant feet, looking this way and that with small, jerky movements of his head, like a chicken on a secret mission. He bore a slim manila file. He saw me watching from my desk, smiled with relief, and approached.

"John," he said, "I thought I'd find you here."

I wagged my pencil at him. "That's because it's the detectives' room, and I am a detective."

He smiled as though he knew it was a joke but wasn't sure why it was funny. Dehan glanced at me from under her eyebrows then smiled at the inspector.

"Good morning, sir."

"Carmen!" He looked at her in what you could only describe as alarm. "Naturally I was looking for you both! I just happened to see . . ." He swallowed and changed tack. "I like to get out of my office from time to time, see the troops, haha . . ."

I smiled amiably. "Here we are, sir, trooping."

"Indeed! And what are you working on?"

I gestured at the old cartons on the desk. "We were just looking through the cold cases, sir. We were thinking about the

Vince Wolowitz case. They found him tied to his bed in his house on St. Lawrence Avenue."

Dehan nodded. "Clason Point, near the Catholic church. His dog had eaten his foot."

The inspector winced. I contributed, "The neighbors said he had a hundred grand in a box under his bed, but it was never found."

Dehan sat back. "August ninety-seven. I always had a theory about his family."

I wagged my pencil at her. "I've been meaning to look into that angle for some time."

The inspector's smile had turned to a rictus, which is not a good thing to happen to a smile.

"If you haven't started on it yet, I wonder if you would have a look at the Jose Robles case?" he said.

Dehan frowned. "That's cold? What'd they do, keep it in the fridge overnight?"

"I think what Detective Dehan means, sir . . ."

"I know what she means, John, and she is quite right." He pulled a chair over from Mo's desk and sat heavily. "The case is not even a week old. But it has run into some . . ." He hesitated, then plunged on. ". . . well, *problems,* which seem intractable. And frankly, I am under pressure from 'above'"—he made little inverted commas with his fingers—"to get it solved 'pronto.'" He did it again, hunching his shoulders a little. "You two," he said, gazing out the window, "seem to have a way of unearthing clues that don't appear even to be there."

"Why thank you, sir." I smiled. "I think so too."

"So, I know it's not strictly a cold case, but I'd be grateful if you'd have a look at it."

He tossed the file in front of me on the desk, and I leaned over and picked it up. "Who had it to start with?"

"Gutierrez, but he's glad to let it go because, as far as *he's* concerned, it's closed. And I have to say . . ."

He hesitated again. Dehan frowned at him. She said, "You

agree . . ." He shrugged. She pressed him. "So why are we looking at it? What is the intractable problem?"

He sighed. "ADA Costas Varoufakis."

Her eyebrows seemed to levitate. "Assistant District Attorney Costas Varu . . . The assistant district attorney is the intractable problem?"

"He does not believe it should be closed."

Suddenly I was interested. I leaned forward. "On what grounds? And since when does the assistant district attorney decide when we close a case?"

"Since his uncle went to school with the mayor."

I grunted. "And his grounds?"

He made a face of helplessness and spread his hands. "It seems they were friends. They shared an interest in Mediterranean history or something."

I made a dubious expression with my eyebrows and offered it to Dehan. She copied it and offered it back. The inspector sighed. "Look, I'm sorry, and I am aware it's an imposition. Just work your magic on it for a day or two, and if you are convinced it's case closed, we close the case and you can get on with . . ."

He made little stirring motions with his finger. I said, "Vince Wolowitz."

"Indeed."

"Of course we will. I shall enter it into my little black book of favors to be called in at a later time, sir."

"He's joking, sir," said Dehan, in a way that said that I wasn't.

He nodded and smiled, and retreated up to the rarified atmosphere of the upper floor. I took the photos from the file and tossed the rest at Dehan. She read as I looked.

"Jose Robles, a Spanish national."

I spoke, looking at a photograph of him. "Spanish from Spain?"

She stared at me a moment. "Yes, Spanish from Spain. PhD in applied physics from the University of Santiago de Compostela, Galicia. That's also in Spanish Spain."

"I know. I've been. Excellent seafood."

"He was conducting research and lecturing at University College New York, in Manhattan. He'd been here a year last September and had another year to run."

The photograph I was looking at was a head and shoulders portrait. I figured he was thirty-something, and he was handsome in that Mediterranean kind of way that women find so appealing: dark, chiseled features, black hair, and big, brown eyes that managed to be both sweet and insolent at the same time. His hair was receding slightly, and the collar of his pink shirt was on the outside of his turquoise cashmere sweater. He wasn't smiling.

Dehan was saying, "He was found December fourth, that's last Tuesday, at the house of a friend, Agnes Shine, also a lecturer at the university. He had been shot eight times in the thorax with a 9mm Sig Sauer Tacops P226..."

We both looked up, stared at each other, and frowned. She raised her eyebrows and went back to reading. I stared at the naked trees outside, then turned back to the photos and found the one of Dr. Jose Robles lying sprawled and dead in an armchair. I was looking at the blood on his chest.

"The weapon was recovered at the scene..."

"Dropped on the floor near the body."

"Correct. It was sent for prints and still awaiting results."

"What about Agnes Shine?"

"I'm coming to that, big guy. She was known to be a close friend of the victim. Dr. Patricia Meigh, Jose's head of department..."

"Me?"

"Meigh, M-E-I-G-H, Meigh, she's the head of the department that was conducting the research that Jose was involved in. She was concerned when Jose didn't turn up Monday morning and wouldn't answer his phone. She tried to locate Agnes Shine, but it turned out she hadn't shown up either..."

"What's her department?"

"Um . . ." She scanned several pages. "Professor of Economics and International Finance."

"Huh, okay."

"She didn't turn up either. Tuesday they were both missing again, so Dr. Meigh raised the alarm. A patrol car was dispatched to his house with no result. Her house is a few doors down, so they went to have a look. Living room is on the second floor, but there are outside stairs. They saw him through the window."

"The drapes were open."

"Presumably."

"They were." I waved the photograph at her.

"Uh-huh. Stephens Avenue, right by Pugsley Creek Park. Officers forced their way in, found the victim deceased at eleven a.m., and no trace of Agnes. No driver's license or any other kind of ID was found at the house. Her purse was also missing, leading Detective Gutierrez to conclude that she had killed Jose in a fit of passion and fled."

"Witnesses?"

"Uniforms canvassed the neighbors, but nobody saw or heard anything out of the ordinary. Jose was last seen by a friend at the university Friday evening at eight. So time of death is sometime between Friday at eight p.m. and Tuesday at eleven in the morning."

She dropped the file and reached across to pick up the photographs. I sat drumming my fingers on the desk and gazing at the stark, gray sky outside. "It has, as Holmes would say, some interesting features. Was the Sig registered to either of them?"

She answered while staring at the photograph of Jose Robles, dead in the chair. "Nope. Unregistered."

"Curiouser and curiouser."

"You're mixing your quotes. That's *Alice in Wonderland*."

I stood and grabbed my coat. "Come, Dehan, I want to have a look at the crime scene. For once it is less than ten years old. It might actually tell us something."

"I'm giddy with excitement," she said with no particular

expression and gathered up the papers and photographs into the file.

She pulled on a thick coat, a brown-and-white angora wool hat, and matching gloves, and we went to collect the keys to the properties. Then we made our way out into the ice-cold street. There was no snow, but what moisture there was on the roads had frozen and had the brittle look of thin ice. We crossed to my ancient Jaguar—an authentic, right-hand-drive, burgundy Mark II from 1964, with leather seats and walnut trim—and climbed in. As we slammed the doors, shutting out the icy air, Dehan said, "I can see why Varou . . . the ADA."

"Varoufakis."

I fired up the engine and reversed out of the lot. Dehan was still talking.

"I can see why he's not satisfied. A Sig Sauer Tacops P226, new, is going to cost you over a grand. It's a serious pro's weapon, favored by special ops units like the SEALS and Delta Force. You can pick up a Glock 17, which is a damn good gun, for half the price. Or a Taurus, which is okay, for half that again. So what is Dr. Agnes Shine doing with a thousand-buck weapon that isn't registered to her, or anybody else?"

I turned from Story onto Soundview and made a "hmmm . . ." noise. "Did you look at the photograph of him?"

"Which one?"

"The portrait." She watched me but didn't say anything. "He looks to me like the kind of man who might own an expensive gun. Possibly he wouldn't own a gun, but if he did, he would buy an expensive one."

"You can tell that from his portrait photograph?"

"Sure. You don't believe me? What is the betting he drove a German car?"

"*What . . . ?*"

"Come on, what do *you* think he drove?"

"I have no idea, Stone."

"Audis are too common for him, likewise Mercedes, and VW. Porsche is out of his price range. BMW. The three-twenty, in . . ."

"Come on!"

"Wait—in white."

"That's ridiculous."

"Not at all. He wears a pink shirt with a turquoise cashmere sweater, and he has the collar on the outside. That kind of thing can tell you a lot about a man and his relationship with his mother: he is vain, showy, has poor judgment, bad taste, and he believes he is entitled to the best because Mommy told him so."

She sighed and shook her head. "Anyway, okay, so maybe the gun was his. Still, it is odd that it was not registered."

"Laws are pretty tight here. Still, I take your point, if he had one, you'd expect it to be legal. By the way, what did you think about the picture of him in the chair, shot?"

She leafed through them till she'd found it. She was quiet for a moment, examining it.

"Not a lot. They'd been drinking. He has a glass of wine beside him." She leafed through them again and looked at another picture. "There is another glass on the table beside the sofa. They were both sent for fingerprinting, and the bottle."

"What's the wine?"

"The wine?"

"Yes, what is it? California, Chile, French . . . ?"

She peered at the picture. "It looks like . . . Bogle Vineyards, 2016. Is that important?"

"California. It might be, Little Grasshopper."

"Whatever . . . It was sent for fingerprinting too. What else? Nothing much. Why? Am I missing some cigarette ash or something? Are you going to identify the killer by the texture of the burned paper?"

"That vitriol which is drooling from your lips, Detective Dehan, will come back to burn you in the ass. We are here."

I pulled into Patterson Avenue and, as we crossed into

Compton and Stephens, we were suddenly in a country village somewhere in New England. I smiled. "I love these little corners of the Bronx, don't you, Dehan? You're in this vast city, with millions of people around you, and yet you could be in rural Maine."

She cocked an eyebrow at me. "Is this what they call being whimsical, Stone? Are you feeling whimsical today? You haven't got a craving for tinned peaches and oysters, have you? Tell me you're not pregnant."

I chortled good-humoredly and slowed outside a large clapboard house on three floors plus an attic, with yellow tape across the porch. The house was part of a row of four that were all oddly grotesque but somehow managed to be attractive. Everywhere about them was a superabundance of foliage from the woodland in the park at the back of the houses.

"That's his house, right?"

"Uh-uh. Hers is the first on the left, after the trees, about two hundred yards down."

Agnes' house was, like all the houses on Stephens Avenue, peculiar. It was set behind a chain-link fence and gate, beyond a large lawn that must have been thirty yards long at the very least, and a good fifteen yards across. Like Jose's house, it was clapboard but seemed to be put together from bits that were left over from other clapboard houses.

It had a gable roof and also a flat roof, an arch over a carport, a chimney that ran all the way up the outside of the house, right beside the front door, and a flight of six substantial stone steps up to that door. I was still trying to work out how the fireplace could be next to the front door when I noticed a broad flight of wooden steps going up to the second story, on the outside of the carport. It was like something from the Picasso school of abstract architecture.

Here too there was yellow tape across the chain-link fence, and also across the front porch. We climbed out, and the slam of the car doors echoed across the icy morning. A couple of ravens, scared by the reports, flapped darkly away toward Pugsley Creek

Park. The lawn was well tended, the frosty grass was short and was obviously mowed regularly, but there were no flower beds, no trees, no bench for sitting out in the evening.

We crossed the front yard. Dehan pulled away the tape from the door, unlocked it, and we stepped inside. It was dark, and there was a silence in the place that comes with death. It was a quiet saturated with stillness. The door that had mystified me turned out to be the kitchen door. The kitchen, along with the dining area, took up the whole of the ground floor, and the chimney I'd seen from the car was a flue that rose from an old, blue iron range that stood to the right as you went in. It looked like an antique, and it was spotless.

The floors were hardwood and highly polished. There was a table in the middle of the floor with four chairs placed evenly around it. A doily in the exact center held a vase of plastic flowers. There was an oak dresser against one wall that also appeared to be an antique. Beside it, a wine rack held twenty-four bottles of wine. I examined them. They were all Spanish, twelve from Rioja and twelve from Ribera del Duero.

After that, I went methodically through the drawers. They were well ordered and, like everything else in the kitchen, very clean. Dehan was watching me with her hands in her back pockets.

"What are you looking for?"

"Agnes Shine."

"You think she's hiding in the cutlery drawer?"

"This house belongs to a highly ordered eccentric who doesn't like high-maintenance relationships."

She smiled and pulled off her hat. "You're something, Stone."

"No flowers." I pointed at the vase. "Plastic."

An arch in the left-hand wall gave onto a narrow entrance with a door into the carport and a flight of stairs that led to the upper floor. These were wood too, and carpeted in an ugly dark green. They creaked as we climbed.

On the upper floor, there was a landing. At the back, there

were two bedrooms and a bathroom. The front of the house was taken up by a large living room. Here there was an open fireplace with a white marble surround. Another antique. Two tall windows overlooked the long lawn and the street. There were low, heavy wooden bookcases along all the walls, holding books on just about everything, but there was no fiction. Nor were there ornaments, nor pictures on the walls. There were four large, attractive lamps, evenly spaced, and a single overhead bulb with a green shade.

An old television was positioned in the corner, near the fireplace. Opposite, there was a brown sofa upholstered in suede. On either side, at an angle, there were two matching armchairs. One of them was caked with dry blood and peppered with small, black holes.

The silence was total.

Dehan pointed at the windows. "Triple glazing. Probably why the neighbors didn't hear anything."

I nodded and took my pen from my inside pocket. I crouched down beside the chair and slipped my pen into three of the bullet holes. Dehan said, "What?"

I shook my head and made a "nothing" face, then stood. "The sofa and the chairs, they are based on the design of Coco Chanel's sofa at the Ritz. They are very good imitations. That's buffalo hide. You're looking at sixty thousand bucks' worth of furniture right there, Dehan."

"Sixty grand?"

I nodded. "So he's sitting in that chair. He's got a glass of wine on that table, beside him. According to the photograph, she's probably sitting on that chair on the other side of the sofa, because that's where the other glass was, and the bottle. Does that seem odd to you?"

"A little." She shrugged. "But she's mad at him, remember? Usually they'd probably both be snuggled up on the sofa, watching a movie or something. But today she's mad at him. So they're a bit uptight, formal, they're sitting on chairs having what he thinks is going to be an adult conversation to sort out their problems. Instead, she's got this Sig."

I nodded. "She's got it here, concealed somewhere, ready to shoot him, or maybe she's left it in her room. She's thinking if he comes through, she'll forgive him. But he doesn't, he just makes her mad, so she gets up, goes to her room, collects the weapon, comes back, and lets rip."

"Eight shots, that's a pretty mad woman."

"Yeah. From the photograph, I'd say she was standing here, in the middle of the floor."

I positioned myself halfway between the two chairs, about seven or eight feet from where Jose had been sitting. Dehan frowned. "So that looks like she went and got the gun, right? Because if she was sitting in the other chair, where her glass was, why would she get up and go over there to shoot him? And, if she had, he would have got up, tried to run or take the gun. So like you said, she's left the room, got the weapon, and come back to where you are, and shot him."

I nodded slowly, looked around the room, and stared at Dehan. "There are several things troubling me, Dehan, but you know what's troubling me the most?"

She smiled. "No, but two gets you twenty it'll be something that annoys me."

"I can't even *smell* a motive."

TWO

She pulled off her coat, walked away, and stood staring out at the street. Her silhouette against the cold, gray light was long and slim. After a moment, she turned and sat on the windowsill.

"They were close. They were probably having an affair. He was going to ditch her, or there was another woman—story as old as hormones. We don't know anything about them yet."

"I know . . ." I looked around the room. "But does this look to you like a place where there was a crime of passion? Even the wineglasses have coasters."

"What are you getting at?"

"I don't know. The wineglasses have coasters, everything is neat and tidy, and yet she has blown eight holes in her twenty-thousand-dollar suede chair. And she has used a silencer."

"How the hell do you know that? There's triple glazing . . ."

"A fact which she would have known. But the penetration, from a 9mm Sig, there would have been deeper penetration into the chair, I think. The silencer reduces the velocity of the bullet."

I crossed the landing to the bedroom. The drapes were closed. They too were a dark green, and thin cracks of green light glowed down their sides from the park woodland outside. The bed was made and uncreased. I went into the en suite bathroom. There was a shower cubicle, but no bath. The towels were all folded and clean. There was a shower gel scented with lime and lavender, and an anti-frizz shampoo for extra body. And there were a lot of other things I had started to find in my own bathroom since I had married Dehan.

I stepped out of the bathroom and saw Dehan with her arms crossed, leaning against the doorjamb, looking down at the bed.

"I know what you mean," she said. "There is no disorder."

"The only disorder is the killing." I thought a moment. "The killing, and the fact that she is missing. We may find she's a little OCD when we talk to her workmates."

"Mm-hm. I think you're right."

"This place has nothing to tell me, Dehan. Which, in itself, says something, but I'm not sure what yet. Let's take a walk and see what his house has to say."

We stepped out into the cold, still air and walked, hunched into our coats, the two hundred yards back up the road to Jose Robles' house. This house was, again, peculiar. The first floor was made of raw stone, like big rocks cemented together then filed down so they were flat. It was indescribably ugly. A flight of steps, which looked like something out of a medieval castle, rose to the front door, not directly, but across the facade of the house; and that front door was not at ground level, but on the second floor. The third floor and the attic were all clapboard, like the back of the house.

As we approached, breathing great clouds of condensation, Dehan, whose nose and cheeks had turned red under her hat, said, "Do you think these houses were designed in the sixties, and the architects were all high on acid?"

"It would explain a lot."

We turned in off the sidewalk and headed for the stairs. Just to the left of them was a double garage. I stopped, took hold of Dehan's elbow, and pointed. She stared, then looked me in the face and emitted a high-pitched laugh, which she kept going all the way up the steps to the front door. The reason for her laughter was the white BMW 320 which was parked outside the garage.

She opened the door and we went in. The front door gave directly onto the living room. It was a style that in the late '60s and early '70s would have been considered modern. The walls were paneled in tongue and groove, the fireplace was stone, and the furniture was all low and leather, though none of it was of the class or quality of Agnes' stuff.

There were many lamps, of all kinds of shapes and sizes, mostly pretentious and all of it expensive. There was a large coffee table in the middle of the floor that seemed to be made out of hunks of driftwood, and there were books, lots of them, stuffed into every available nook and cranny. Most of them were in Spanish, but a good number of professional reference books were in English. Open on the table was the *Journal of the Electrochemical Society*. I picked it up and had a look at what he was reading: "The Development and Future of Lithium Ion Batteries," by George E. Blomgren. It didn't mean much to me. I put it back down and continued looking around. He had a well-stocked bar, and there was a lot of soot in the fire.

I pointed at the alcoves on either side of the fire, where cabinets and shelves had been put in. "Unlike her, he has photographs."

She moved over and started looking at them, muttering, "Yeah, Agnes didn't have any. That was odd."

I went and hunkered down by the fire. I took the poker from the stand and started poking around in the soot. There were still a few hunks of blackened wood that had not burned completely. I stood and looked at his collection of bottles. He had Tio Pepe dry sherry, Martini, Gordon's Gin, Beefeater, Glenfiddich Scotch whiskey, and Johnnie Walker Red Label.

Dehan spoke suddenly, still looking at the photographs. "Looks like his family. That looks like his mother and his father and a bunch of friends. They're cooking paella out in the country. That guy has to be his brother."

I stood and looked over her shoulder. "Why?"

"Looks like him, and he's in these pictures too. The Spanish are Mediterranean, they are very family oriented. Look, see that pretty girl there? She looks like me. That's his sister."

I ruffled her head and told her she was cute and made my way across the large room into the kitchen. There was no door separating the two rooms; it was just another space, sectioned off.

A heavy crystal tumbler stood beside the sink. I picked it up and smelled it. It smelled of whiskey. I opened the dishwasher. There was nothing inside it. He had a big, silver fridge and beside it a wine rack. Like Agnes', it held two dozen bottles in it, mainly red, all from Rioja or Ribera del Duero in Spain.

I leaned my ass against the work surface and crossed my arms. Dehan walked in. I scratched my Adam's apple.

"It was cold. He had a fire burning, yet her drapes were open. He was drinking whiskey and reading his journal. Somebody or something disturbed him. He set down his journal and brought his empty glass to the kitchen, then, presumably, made his way to Agnes' house. There they drank wine and she shot him, with a suppressed Sig, while the drapes were open."

"It is odd. I see where the ADA is coming from. We need Robles' phone records, and hers, see if she called him. If we can establish that she called him over the weekend, that will help narrow down time of death. I'll get on that." As an afterthought, she added, "The lab has his cell."

She walked away dialing and I made my way up to the next floor, to the bedrooms and the bathrooms. There was a landing that ran from front to back. At the far end, the passage made a dogleg and a further flight rose to the attic.

There were three bedrooms. Two were clearly guest rooms and had signs of having been used occasionally, perhaps by his Mediterranean family-oriented family. His room, the master bedroom, had red satin sheets on the bed, a Spanish translation of a Stephen King novel on the bedside table, and an electronic clock with an alarm set for six a.m. In a laundry basket he had some dirty linens, including more sheets. These were in black satin.

I checked his wardrobe and found a handful of good, off-the-peg suits, several pairs of Levi's, several cashmere sweaters in dubious colors, and lots of expensive shirts. His shoes were real leather and handmade. There was nothing else.

I explored both bathrooms. There was nothing of interest there either. I sat on the stairs and thought about that and decided that, like at Agnes' house, the absence of anything interesting was interesting in itself. Downstairs I could hear Dehan talking. When she had finished, I rose and made my way down. She met me at the foot of the stairs. There we stood, staring at each other as I sucked my teeth.

"If they were lovers, Dehan, and I am not saying they weren't, they had a very sterile, clinical relationship. There is no sign of his presence in her house, and no sign of her presence in his house. Where the hell did they have sex? Unless they had a third dwelling somewhere, where they used to meet up and get all their primal urges out of their system, these kids were not involved with each other. Not in any meaningful sense of the word."

She was staring at me with narrowed eyes. "I know," she said. "I was thinking the same thing. But if they weren't involved, why the hell did she kill him?"

I shrugged. "There is always the other Big Motive."

"Money?"

"What else? Or, it may not have been her. Gutierrez assumes it was her because she has vanished, but we haven't got the prints back yet. We don't know if her prints are on the gun or not."

"That's true. She may have vanished because she's dead."

I sighed and shook my head. "But that does present us with a different problem. When people kill for money, or power, it tends to be premeditated and more or less carefully planned. When people pump other people full of lead, drop the weapon, and run, that tends to be a killing motivated by rage, jealousy, vengeance—sex. Something that makes you temporarily lose control."

She slapped me on the shoulder. "Let's go talk to Frank, drop in on the lab while we're there." She opened the door and we stepped out into the icy morning again. "Did you look at the lock at Agnes' place?"

"Yup." I thrust my hands in my pockets as we made our way down the castle steps and started walking back toward the car. "It wasn't forced. And as Jose was not actually at his own house, that means either A, the killer was a third party and Agnes let him in, or B, it was Agnes."

"Him or her." She said it after a long silence as she walked around the car with her hands in her pockets, her shoulders hunched and her collar up, then sniffed. We climbed in and slammed the doors. I turned the key and the big old engine roared into life.

"We should also remember," I said, "that they are both academics. And academics are all more or less crazy."

She was nodding as I pulled away and headed toward White Plains Road. "This is a guy who sits down in front of the fire, with a glass of single malt, and reads about batteries."

We took it easy, and, twenty minutes later, we found Frank in his office, behind a steel desk, going through papers. He looked up as we came in, frowned, and said, "What?"

Dehan sat without being invited. She still had her hands in her pockets and her shoulders hunched. I stayed in his doorway and smiled at him.

"Good morning, Frank. Jose Robles, multiple gunshot wounds to the chest, Stephens Avenue..."

"I know who Jose Robles is, John. I thought Gutierrez had that case. Surely it hasn't gone cold already! I haven't even sent him my results yet!"

"It's the weather, Frank. It's making everything cold. We got handed the case. What can I tell you? Or, more to the point, what can you tell us?"

He shook his head at Dehan across the desk. "It's his wit that makes him so endearing."

He finished shuffling papers and stood, went to an "out" tray on top of a filing cabinet, took a manila envelope, and handed it to Dehan.

"We haven't got a sample of Agnes Shine's fingerprints, but from samples taken from her office and her house, we have isolated some prints that offer an extremely high probability of being hers. They are, however, suggestive and not admissible as evidence."

Dehan nodded and reluctantly extracted a hand from her pocket to take the envelope. "Obviously," she said.

"What can I tell you?" He sighed. "The gun, a Sig Sauer Tacops P226, an unusual choice for a crime of passion. Based on the prints, it was fired by the person we assume to be Agnes Shine. We can say with absolute certainty that the person who fired the gun was a frequent visitor to Agnes' office and her home, almost certainly her. She also handled the bottle and one of the glasses found at the scene."

He dropped back into his chair. "What else? There is very little else. He was shot eight times at close range. He could have died from any one of the wounds, which perforated his liver, his stomach, his lungs, and his heart . . ."

I leaned my shoulder on the doorjamb. "But the one that killed him was the one to the heart."

"Indeed."

"So I guess you haven't examined the contents of his stomach."

He managed to scowl and raise an eyebrow at the same time. "Can you think of a reason why I would have?"

I nodded. "Yeah, I'd like to know what he had for his last supper."

"You're serious."

"I am."

"Anything else you'd like me to waste the taxpayers' dollars on?"

"No . . . I'd be curious to know if he'd had sex before getting shot, but my other questions are for Joe."

He frowned. "Really? I don't know what you're looking for, John, but I have seen many crimes of passion in my time, and this murder is entirely consistent."

"Almost. Have a look in his belly for me, will you?"

"What do you mean, 'almost'?"

I smiled. "Well, there's the gun, and then there's the sequence of the shots."

Dehan turned in her chair to stare at me. The expression on her face was an echo of the one on Frank's. He said, "Sequence? What sequence?"

Dehan shrugged. "What sequence, Stone?"

"The shot to the heart, the one that killed him, was also the first shot."

"Excuse me?"

"None of the other wounds bled anywhere near as profusely. The first shot stopped his heart pumping. So the first shot, delivered with a suppressed Sig Sauer P226—the pro's choice—hit him in the heart and killed him."

Dehan blinked a lot. Frank sighed. "Is there anything else you'd like to tell me? The person who pulled the trigger on that gun has a ninety-nine-point-nine percent chance of being Dr. Agnes Shine. Now go away, please."

I smiled and looked at my watch. "We'd better leave before I upset him. We need to go and see Dr. Meigh, and on the way I need to call Joe."

Frank shrugged. "Joe'll tell you the same thing." To Dehan he said, "I only work with him. You married him."

On the way out, I tossed Dehan the keys. "Let's go see Dr. Meigh."

She climbed behind the wheel, and I got in the passenger seat and called Joe at the lab as she pulled out of the lot and onto Morris Park Avenue.

"Yeah?"

"Joe, it's Stone. Listen, I just got handed the Jose Robles case."

"Okay, how can I help?"

"I need you to have a look at his sheets."

"*His* sheets?"

"Yeah, from his house. He has some dirty sheets in his linen basket, also the stuff on the bed, pillows, duvet, everything."

"I'm looking for signs of sexual activity?"

"Exactly. And, while you're at it, the same with the bedding from Agnes Shine's place."

"Okay, I'll get a team over there."

"And Joe, I also need you to look for traces of saliva on the glasses. I want to know who drank from them."

"You got it."

I hung up and Dehan said, "We don't know who drank from those glasses?"

"Not for a fact, no. In fact, the outstanding feature about this case is Agnes Shine's absence. Gutierrez assumed she was there because Jose Robles was at her house. Now Frank has added a series of fingerprints to the equation, which we *assume* were made by her. But we don't know for a fact that she made them, do we? And I keep coming back to the same thing: we cannot find even a remote trace of a motive. There is no indication that Agnes and Jose were anything but friends and colleagues."

She screwed up her brow and made a "hmmm" noise. "I don't know, Stone. This may be what in Spanish they call looking for five legs on the cat. The cat's got four legs, not five."

"Yeah, I know, Occam's razor. But frankly, I'm having trouble finding even three legs on this cat. At risk of taxing the metaphor, this cat walks like a duck and quacks like a goose. I keep playing this movie in my head. He's sitting there, in front of the fire, sipping his single malt, reading about batteries, and what happens? The phone rings or somebody knocks at the door."

"It might have been a prior arrangement."

"It might have been. In any case, he leaves his magazine open and he takes his glass to the kitchen." I turned to her. "Did you notice the kitchen? It was spotless. There weren't even dirty plates in the dishwasher. But he leaves the glass by the sink and he walks the two hundred yards to Agnes' house . . ."

Dehan started talking, staring ahead through the windshield.

"She lets him in, they sit in this very formal way, with the whole sofa between them, sipping a glass of wine each. Then she gets up, goes to the bedroom, takes this gun from somewhere, and shoots him, eight rounds, in a kind of frenzy."

"Yeah, the kind of frenzy where the first shot scores a bull's-eye."

She sighed. "You're right. The rage does seem to come out of left field for no particular reason."

"If I was that mad at someone that I was going to shoot them, I'd confront them on their doorstep. Or if I'd brought them to my house, I wouldn't fix them up with a drink first. The whole setup looks so formal."

She shrugged as she turned onto Boston Road. "Like you said, Stone. They're academics. Maybe they're just weird."

"Maybe. Let's see what Dr. Meigh says."

THREE

"They were both a bit weird, to be perfectly honest, Detectives."

Dr. Patricia Meigh was surprisingly small, though her presence was surprisingly large. She sat in her black leather chair, behind her oak desk, like a much bigger woman, and turned her black Parker fountain pen over in her fingers. I frowned.

"Were?"

"Forgive me." She didn't smile. "He was. She, no doubt, continues to be, wherever she is."

Dehan asked, "Weird in what way, exactly?"

She studied her pen a moment, pursing her lips. "You know the big difference between scientists and doctors, or engineers?"

"I have often wondered," I lied.

"For doctors and engineers, it's all about fixing a problem—a *real* problem. The engineer wants to get it built, get it made, put together. The doctor wants to cure her patient, make people well. But for scientists, it's all about proving the hypothesis. They exist in the abstract. They dream up a theory, work out how they can turn the theory into an hypothesis, and they are happy, satisfied, when they can prove the hypothesis is correct. That was Jose and that was Agnes. They both existed—and she presumably continues to exist—in theoretical, hypothetical worlds." She hesitated a moment. "Agnes wasn't strictly a scientist, of course, but a mathematician. Her work was entirely theoretical, in any case."

Dehan gave a small grunt and squinted at Meigh. "That's pretty vague, Dr. Meigh. Can you be more precise?"

"Yes, I can be very precise. They were both completely inept socially. At any kind of social gathering, she would go and stand in a corner and stare, completely unnoticed, while he would butt into other people's conversation and talk incessantly about himself. The man's ego, and his vanity, knew no limits, whereas she is a zero personality. She is a void, an empty space. Quite brilliant, truly, but absolutely no ego." She added, with a touch of bitterness, "They were made for each other."

Dehan looked up from a prolonged study of her thumbs. "So they *were* involved with each other?"

"Oh, good heavens, yes! Involved with each other and, more precisely, involved *in* each other. They went everywhere together, did everything together, forever united in this kind of ghastly, joyless bond. The Jose Robles admiration society, membership of two: him and his slave." A trace of a smile flitted across her face. "I am exaggerating, but not very much."

"Did he talk much about Spain?"

Dehan glanced at me like she thought the question was weird, but Dr. Meigh rolled her eyes and said, "*Incessantly!* Nothing was as good as it was in Spain, especially the food. He was forever moaning about American food, as though all we ever ate was hamburgers. Spanish food was the best in the world. Everything Spanish was the best!"

"Yes, I noticed they both had a lot of Rioja and Ribera del Duero."

"No doubt, whatever that is. Forgive my being blunt, but he was a supreme pain in the ass. And a male chauvinist to go with it: what he used to call the *macho ibérico*. The Iberian macho, a strutting, pompous little . . ." She paused and breathed in noisily through her nose. "I guess I shouldn't really talk about him like that to the cops, huh?"

She smiled and I returned it. "Actually, it is very helpful. We were having some difficulty getting a handle on who they were, and their relationship with each other."

"They were very close," she said. "I have no idea what she saw in him. I am very fond of Agnes. I have known her for a long time and mentored her as an academic. She is a highly intelligent woman, but she has a very weak ego, and he neutralized her completely. I am not a psychologist, but I could see that there was some kind of codependent relationship developing there. It was a shame." She narrowed her eyes and made a kind of claw with her right hand. "He seemed to be *consuming* her. He even rented a house in the same street so he could be close to her and they could come to work together and go home together. I suspect he wanted to control her."

Dehan sat back in her chair. "Were you and she close? Did she ever talk to you about him, them . . ."

She made a dubious face. "She was as close to me as she was to anybody, except Jose, but she never discussed their relationship with me. Whatever they had going on, they were never demonstrative in public. They never hugged or kissed or anything like that." She sat forward suddenly and pointed at her own chest. "*I'd* hug her sometimes, because I felt so goddamn sorry for her! She was hungry for love and affection, you could tell that. But with him it was always me, me, me, and I'm the greatest and Spain is the best damn country in the world. Got on my nerves, I don't mind telling you."

I scratched my cheek and sucked my teeth. "Was he good? As a scientist?"

"Very good. More than very good. He was brilliant. He was on his way to big things."

"You were his boss?"

She smiled like I'd said something quaint. "Doesn't really

work like that. He was conducting research under my supervision, in my department."

"What was the research?"

"I can only tell you in very broad terms, Detective. Obviously it is highly confidential, but in essence, he was conducting research into lithium-ion batteries."

"Next big thing?"

She gave her head a little jerk to the side and raised her eyebrows. "It could lead to a transformation as huge as the Industrial Revolution, or bigger. But I really can't discuss it."

I nodded. "Sure, I understand. And whatever research he conducted would be the property of the university."

"Those are the standard terms of the contract." She frowned. "But I don't see what that can have to do with Agnes killing Jose. They weren't even in the same department. Her work was related to socioeconomic dynamics and the impact of international finance on cultural development."

Dehan spoke suddenly, glancing at me like she agreed with Dr. Meigh and wanted to get the conversation back on track. "You said you were about as close to Agnes as anyone. Have you any idea where she might have gone?"

She shook her head. "I'm sorry, Detective Dehan, none whatsoever. We simply weren't *that* close. I was a friend to her in that I was supportive, but she really never confided in me in any way." She gave a small laugh. "If she has any sense, she's in the Bahamas!"

Dehan grunted and muttered, "Or Goa," then asked, "Was there anyone, besides Jose, that she was close to?"

"No. I don't honestly think she confided in anyone. Jose, maybe, if he were able to listen."

"How about family?"

She smiled. "You're out of luck. She was an only child. Father died when she was a young child, drank himself to death. Mother was an art teacher, if I recall. A rather indolent, negligent woman.

She died a few years back. Agnes inherited the house from her. I am not aware of any other family."

Dehan grunted, then sighed. "How about rivals, Doctor? The way you've described them, they don't sound like very attractive people, but is it possible that Jose had started seeing somebody else?"

She gave a derisive little snort. "It's possible, I suppose. Frankly, I find it hard to believe any woman would go for a man like that, but I am constantly amazed at the specimens some women are attracted to. He may well have been seeing someone else. I am just not aware of it. But please don't get me wrong about Agnes. She is a very sweet person once you get to know her."

I made to stand. "Who has his class now, Doctor?"

"Donald, Donald Hays." She glanced at her watch. "He should be finishing his lecture now, two floors down, in the Goodenough Theater."

I glanced at Dehan. She shrugged and shook her head. I stood.

"Dr. Meigh, thank you for your time. You have been very helpful." She stood, we shook hands, and I opened the door. As Dehan stepped out, I turned to Meigh and asked her, "By the way, which one are you? A doctor or a scientist?"

She looked surprised. "Me? Neither! I'm an academic. All I want is the corner office with the best view, the best parking lot, and a towering reputation."

"Oh." I laughed. "Is that what an academic is? I had often wondered."

I closed the door, and we made our way down two floors in the elevator. After a moment, Dehan frowned at me. "The Goodenough Theater?"

"John Goodenough. He invented the lithium-ion battery."

"Why do you know that?"

I raised an eyebrow. "Why don't you?"

We found Donald Hays leaving the Goodenough Lecture Theater. He was a lean man in his early forties with a big black briefcase, a big, domed head, and balding hair that grew long over his collar. His students streamed about him like a river that has broken its banks, and he was pushing through them like a man trying to escape a flood. He was easy to identify.

"Mr. Hays?" I showed him my badge as the students milled around us. "NYPD. This is Detective Dehan, I am Detective Stone."

He seemed to sag. "Is it about Jose?"

"Yes. Have you somewhere we can go?"

"I have half an hour for lunch. Can we talk in the cafeteria? It's downstairs."

He led us down to the cafeteria at a brisk pace that was hard to keep up with, his head down and his legs moving fast, as though he hoped not to be noticed. As we pushed through the glass doors into the spacious, soulless, self-service canteen, he pointed across the room at a table by the glass wall overlooking Washington Square Village and said, "That's my table. Grab my table. I'll get the coffee. You want coffee?"

We crossed the room, which was hung with a few listless baubles and bits of tinsel, grabbed his table, and sat, watching him load his tray. Dehan dumped her woolen hat on the table and ran her fingers through her hair. "All academics are like this," she pronounced, like she was passing judgment. "They're all crazy. My cousin is a lecturer in the classics. He's the same. Neurotic. Everything is an issue. They're all out of their minds."

"Your cousin is a lecturer in the classics?"

"You never met my family."

"You won't let me."

"I'm afraid you'll judge me."

"That's crazy."

"You see? You're doing it already."

Hays approached with his tray, put it down on the table, and handed out the coffees. As he set about peeling the plastic off his chicken sandwich, he said, "They're fifty cents each."

I gave him a dollar. "How well did you know Jose Robles, Mr. Hays?"

"It's Dr. Hays, and I imagine they have told you already, we were quite close." He bit into his sandwich. Picked up his cup, put it down again, and spoke with his mouth full. "But not close enough to kill him, for God's sake."

He made a face that might have been a smile, tried to sip his coffee, winced, and took another bite from his sandwich.

"Did you socialize?"

He swallowed so he could answer. "Well, I mean, how else would you be close to somebody? Short of moving in together." He gave a small laugh. "And we weren't that close. So we used to go out sometimes. Have a drink and sometimes a meal. And we would talk. That is how you become close, I think."

Dehan leaned her elbows on the table. "Were you close with both of them, or just Jose?"

"I knew Agnes long before Jose came on the scene. We sometimes had lunch together. Like me, she preferred the student cafeteria. At least here people don't stab you in the back . . ." He made a stabbing gesture with his hand, to illustrate. "While you're quietly having your chicken sandwich, as it is today. But it was only when Jose—he liked to be called Pepe, funny story, I'll tell you later—came along, that we started actually *going out*. He was very gregarious. He missed the Spanish nightlife."

She smiled and narrowed her eyes. "Was that just the three of you, or did more people tag along?"

"Mainly it was just us. But sometimes he would go with other people. He was pretty popular. Everybody liked him. He was noisy. People like noisy, I think."

"Noisy?"

He took two bites of his sandwich and nodded. "Mm-hm." He swallowed, reached for his coffee again, but didn't pick it up. "Talked loud. Never stopped."

I scratched my forehead. "Dr. Hays, I need you to think very carefully about this. Is it possible that Jose was seeing another woman, besides Agnes?"

"Why do I have to think carefully about that? It's not a complicated question, Detective. By seeing, I assume you mean having sexual intercourse."

"Yes, that's what I mean. Was he?"

He gave a half smile. "Obviously, I have never been inside his bedroom, which would be a place forbidden to me. But deducing from the signals that people send each other, which they think are secret but are plainly obvious to anyone bothering to watch, I would say that Dr. Robles was involved in a sexual relationship with Ali."

Dehan's eyebrows shot up. "*Ali?*"

Hays swallowed the last of his sandwich with a smirk, picked up his coffee, and sipped. "Forgive my attempt at humor. It is always funny how people assume that Ali is an Arabic man, when she is in fact a Spanish woman. Alicia, abbreviated to Ali. She lectures in Spanish. He used to joke with us that he indulged in intellectual slumming by hanging out with her, because she was only a linguist, not a scientist. But Agnes didn't think it was funny."

Dehan nodded. "Was she jealous?"

"She was too intelligent to be jealous, but she didn't like it."

"She discussed it with you?"

"We both agreed, we didn't know why he wasted his time with her. She had nothing to say—well, she has lots to say, but none of it was of any interest to anybody with any intelligence. But *they* used to talk together. It was more like shouting. They would both shout at the same time, very loudly, and laugh. I think it reminded them of being at home."

"No doubt. Did either Agnes or Jose ever talk to you about guns? Were you aware that either of them owned a gun?"

He gave a smile that was slightly incredulous. "Why would they own a gun? If they were both anti-gun and anti-violence, against the Second Amendment, why would they own a gun?"

I smiled blandly at him. "Could you answer the question please, Dr. Hays?"

"No, neither of them ever talked about *guns*! I have to go. Can I go?"

"Of course, thank you for your help, Doctor."

He didn't say anything. He just stood, picked up his black bag, and walked out of the cafeteria on his fast, anxious legs. Dehan sighed as she watched him go.

"Well, that helped to clarify absolutely nothing."

I nodded. "I wouldn't say absolutely nothing. We have a rough idea of who we are dealing with. They are both very clever, very complicated people, one with a deeply repressed ego, and the other with a hugely inflated one. And we have people with very contradictory opinions of Jose. Dr. Meigh seems not to have liked him at all, and yet, according to Hays, he seems to have been popular."

She scrunched up her hat into a ball and watched it bounce open again. "Possibly he was popular because of the American intellectual's infatuation with all things European."

"Ouch." After a moment, I added, "Ali *is* European, and she seems to have been infatuated with him. Or at least, they sought solace in each other. The allure of the familiar in an alien land."

"How poetic."

"Come on, Dehan. Let's go and do some intellectual slumming and have a chat with this mere linguist."

FOUR

The college admin office, which sported a small, plastic Christmas tree on its counter, told us that Dr. Alicia Cobos was not in that day, so we got her telephone number and left. On the way to the car, Dehan pulled her woolen hat down over her ears and then pulled her cell from her pocket. As we climbed into the car, she was dialing.

"Dr. Cobos? Hello, good afternoon. This is Detective Carmen Dehan of the NYPD..."

I started the engine and pulled into the traffic. Dehan smiled, but without much feeling. "Yes, yes, it is a Spanish name . . . Alicia, oh, like your mother. That's nice. Dr. Cobos, we were hoping to talk to you about your colleague, Dr. Jose Robles. Is there any chance you could come in and see us?"

She did a lot of nodding, leaned against the door, licked her lips, and raised an eyebrow at me. All the while, I could hear a voice in the background that belonged to somebody who apparently didn't need to breathe.

"That would be great. Thank you. Two p.m. would be great. Forty-Third Precinct, Story Avenue and Fteley. Thank you. See you then." She hung up. "Man, she can talk! The problem is the ratio of content to volume."

We were quiet for a moment, then I said, "That kind of sums up the case so far."

She made a noise of thinking, followed by a small sideways twitch of her head. "I godda say, Sensei, to me it is looking more and more like what it has looked like right from the start."

"And what is that? A crime of passion?"

She shifted in her seat to look at me. "What was the main problem we had? There was no trace of a relationship visible in either one of their houses. Now we know why. It's not that there wasn't a relationship, it's just that they are weird."

I laughed. "Don't let the thought police catch you saying things like that out loud."

"You know what I mean. They don't express their feelings in the usual way. But you heard them. If there was one thing Dr. Meigh and Hays agreed on, it was the fact that they were emotionally dependent on each other. Only thing is, their needs were different. He needed people to need him, and she just needs him. It's a story that's as old as humanity. Faced with the possibility of being abandoned by him, she freaks out and kills him."

"Where'd she get the gun from?"

"C'mon, Stone. This is America! The land of opportunity. Mail order, a pawn shop, maybe she went to South Dakota for the weekend. It is not hard to get a gun if you are determined." She was quiet for a moment, staring at the limp, pre-Christmas lights outside, then went on. "So it's a Sig, okay, that's odd, but if she's buying secondhand and she doesn't know what she's looking for, maybe that's the first thing that came along."

I gave her a look that was skeptical and said, "Mad professor goes looking for a gun in a pawn shop and comes home with a Sig Sauer Tacops P226? Where shall I begin?"

"Yeah, okay, when you put it like that, it sounds ridiculous."

"And you know why that is?"

"Yeah, because it is ridiculous. But the fact that it is odd she should have that particular gun does not take away from the fact that sexual jealousy is the most likely motive, and that she is the most likely suspect."

I nodded. "That is true."

I parked outside the station house, and while Dehan went inside, I took a walk to the deli on the corner to buy some beef sandwiches and two coffees. When I got back, she was at her desk, going through a sheaf of papers. I put her sandwich and her coffee in front of her and she spoke without looking at me.

"His phone records, and hers. Gutierrez just brought them over." She pointed at a file on my desk. "Also her financials. There it is." She picked up a pencil and circled an entry on the record she was holding, then pushed it across the desk at me. "Saturday night, five past ten. She calls him. The call lasts four minutes." She sat back and put her boots on the desk, pointing at me with the pencil. "He's had his dinner, he's washed up and put everything away because he is that kind of fastidious guy who has to have everything just so. Now he's sitting down in front of the fire, reading about batteries and having a glass of Scotch. The phone rings . . ." She jabbed her pencil at the paper. "It's Agnes, and she wants him to come over because she wants to discuss something with him."

"Hang on." I raised a hand. "So far, what you're saying is indisputable, but we have a problem with what comes next. "We have to accept that this very timid, self-effacing woman has gone out and bought a gun, and now lays on wine for this guy, preparatory to shooting him. It's wrong, it just doesn't scan."

"Because, Sensei, you are making an assumption which is not founded in fact."

"I bet you really enjoyed saying that. What assumption?"

"That she went out and bought the gun. She may have had it all her life. Maybe her daddy gave it to her. We have no idea where that gun came from, but it might just as easily have been sitting in her room for years."

I nodded. "That is true."

"And in that scenario, it does not seem so incredible. She

invites him over. They are having wine, and she asks him what gives with him and Ali. He replies with all the arrogance of the macho he believes himself to be. Maybe he puts Agnes down and humiliates her. Tells her that he plans to get serious with Ali. Whatever he tells her, it pushes her over the edge. She goes to her room, gets the gun . . ."

I sighed. "That is very plausible." I picked up her financial records and waved them at her. "What do you say? Will we find an unexplained outlay of one thousand bucks within two or three weeks of his death?"

She shook her head. "Nope."

I started going through it. "Whether we do or not, we need to establish where that gun came from."

As it was, I found no outlay of a thousand dollars that might have been attributable to Agnes' purchase of a Sig Sauer P226. In fact, the most remarkable thing about Agnes' financial records was, as with everything else about her, the absence of anything remarkable.

At five past two, Alicia Cobos arrived, and I had her shown up to an interview room. We joined her a couple of minutes later. She was an attractive woman in her midthirties. Her black hair was cut short, and she moved her hands a lot when she spoke. She was overdressed and had too much makeup on, but in spite of that, she looked good. As I introduced us and we sat down, Dehan put a paper cup of coffee in front of her.

"I brought you some coffee, just in case."

Dr. Cobos peered into the cup and offered Dehan a thin smile. "Thank you, but this is not coffee." She turned to me. "I teach Spanish at the university, and I make it part of my program to introduce Americans to good coffee, good food, and good wine. Is part of Spanish culture."

She laughed like she'd said something outrageous, reached across the table, and touched my hand. "I am afraid America has terrible food, and *horrible* wine!"

I smiled sweetly at her. "It must have been a comfort for you to have Jose at the university, somebody who shared your cultural background."

She made a face and shrugged. "I have many friends. I am friends with everybody."

"Sure, I can imagine . . ." I paused a moment so she could read whatever she wanted into the comment, then asked, "How close were you and Jose?"

"We was friends. Good friends, but nothing more. Go out, come in, have some drinks with friends, no more."

I leaned forward, confidentially, like we were allies. "I'll be honest with you, Dr. Cobos, we believe that Agnes was in love with Jose . . ."

She did a thing where she tucked her chin into her neck, made her eyes big, and flapped her hands like she was shooing me away, and at the same time emitted a long "Oooooh!" I took this to mean she agreed with me, a lot. "She was crazy! Crazy for him, and crazy. Point!"

"Point?"

Dehan gave a small sigh. "Period."

Cobos ignored us both and stormed on. "She was with him *all the time*! But *all the time*! Never! Never you see him alone! Where you go, you see him with her, at the breakfast, at the lunch, when he is going home, if we going out for the dinner, always she is with him. I say to him, '*Tío!*' We say this in Spanish, is like 'Guy!' I say, '*Tío!* You take her with you everywhere? You take her to the toilet? She is like your dog!' He say to me, 'She is my mascot. She bring me lucky.'"

She emitted a scream of laughter. Dehan nodded and said, with no particular inflection, "That's funny. We've heard that he was a bit *machista*. Would you say that was true?"

She did the thing with the hand again and nodded, pursing her lips. "But a lot! But, he say it in a way that make you laugh. He use to tell me, 'What you doing in the university? Taking a job from a man. You should be at home, cooking, making the cleaning. You are antisocial!'" She laughed. "He is joking, but he is serious." She nodded, and suddenly she was sad. "I miss him. He was a . . ." She searched the walls and the ceiling for the word, then fumbled, ". . . personage . . ."

Dehan said, "A character. He was a character."

"Yes, a character."

"Was he in love with you, Dr. Cobos?"

She flopped back in her chair, took a deep breath, and puffed out her cheeks. "I don't know. Jose was in love with one person." She held up a finger to indicate one person. "He was in love with Jose Robles, himself. He was a . . ." Again she hesitated, looking for the word. "*Narcisista.*"

"Narcissist."

"Yes, but . . ." She hunched her shoulders, spread her hands, and nodded slowly several times. "We have a thing, you know? We laugh a lot, we have good compenetration. He like me, and I like him."

Dehan asked, "So, he never said anything to you about his feelings."

"No."

"Did you ever spend the night together, without Agnes?"

Her cheeks colored. "We . . . Twice, he stay at my apartment. Agnes went home in a taxi."

I said, "She was upset, obviously."

She shrugged elaborately. "Is impossible to tell with Agnes."

Dehan sighed and I scratched my chin. "How did that happen? I'm interested in the scene. Did she say she was going? How did it come about?"

"We went to dinner in a restaurant. Me, Jose, Agnes, Donald, some more people. Donald was another one *always* with Jose. Him and Agnes was crazy. Good, so, after the dinner we having a few drinks, then Jose say, come on, we go dancing!" She screwed up her face, presumably imitating Agnes. "No! No! We go home! We godda work! Tomorrow is Wednesday!" She rolled her eyes. "Americans! So boring! So Donald go home, Chen go home, others go home, but Agnes stay. What we are going to do? Go dancing? Me and Jose and Agnes? Like the three amigos? I think no. So Jose say to Agnes, 'Agnes, go home.'"

Dehan grunted. "Just like that?"

"Yes. He call a taxi, give the address, 'I see you in the morning.' Finish." We were all quiet for a moment, then she spoke suddenly. "And second time was similar. But he say to her, 'I gonna spend the night with Ali, you go home now.' She go, get a taxi, and go home."

I nodded. "That was pretty cruel. He must have known she was in love with him."

She shrugged. "Is her problem."

Dehan smiled. "As it turned out, it was his problem too."

I drummed my fingers on the table for a second, feeling oddly frustrated. "Dr. Cobos, we are nearly done. I just have a couple more questions for you. We are trying to establish how Agnes came to get hold of a gun. Did either Jose or Agnes at any time mention a gun to you?"

The look of horror on her face was so extreme it was almost comical. "No!" she said. "*Never!* Jose hate guns! Always he was criticizing American gun law. He says to his colleagues all the time, 'You have highest murder rate in the world, and you let everybody have guns by mail order! Maybe put two and two together, it makes four!'"

Dehan smiled but left her eyes on hold. "Yeah, shame it's not that easy. Actually the U.S.A. is below the international average for murders, and most murders are committed with knives and bare hands, not guns. So he didn't own or buy a gun."

"No, no, no! He hates guns."

"What about Agnes?"

She raised her hands and hunched her shoulders and made a face only Mediterraneans know how to make. "Ah! I don't know! I speak to her only for say hello! But I think—I *think*—she is not a kind of person who owns a gun! Is just my opinion, eh! I don't know."

Dehan pointed at a pendant Cobos had around her neck and

smiled. "That's a very pretty cross. My mother gave me one very similar. Are you a Catholic?"

"Oh, yes! My mother too, she give it to me, for my communion. God is always with me, taking care of me. I no go to the church every Sunday, but in my heart I am a Catholic and with the Lord. Is important."

"It sure is." She turned to me. "So, Stone, I don't know if you have any more questions . . . ?" I shook my head. She went on, "Summing up, you and Jose were just friends, though you did spend the night together twice, Agnes was aware of that, and as far as you know, neither of them owned a gun?"

"That is correct—as far as I know!"

I stood. "Well, Dr. Cobos, I don't think we need detain you any longer. Thank you for coming in, and maybe try some of the Italian cafés for your coffee. You have a good day."

She left on prancing legs with a swing of her hips and a cute smile. Dehan stared at the empty doorway and chewed her lip. I said, "There's your motive, right there."

She nodded. "And you don't like it any more than I do."

I leaned against the wall and folded my arms. "What's bugging you?"

"It's nothing. It doesn't count, but . . ." She shook her head. "She didn't hit the sack with Jose."

I was surprised, and my eyebrows said so. "Based on what?"

She shook her head again. "I told you, it's nothing. It's stupid, but she's a real, devout Catholic. She wears her cross on the *outside* of her blouse. I know the type. There is no way on God's green Earth she is going to hit the sack with Jose if they are just good friends. I just don't buy it. If they were engaged, *maybe*, but just friends? No way."

I frowned. "Then why the hell would she tell us she had?"

"I don't know, Stone. But I am telling you, sure as eggs is eggs, that woman did not have sex with Jose Robles."

"As sure as eggs is eggs? Really?"

"Shut up. I read it somewhere."

FIVE

Back at my desk, the internal phone buzzed. I answered, and Maria the desk sergeant said, "Hey, lover boy, you got a call on line two."

I smiled at Dehan as she dropped into her chair. "Maria, if Carmen ever catches us, she will surely kill us both."

"Say hi to her for me."

"Maria says hi."

"Tell her to give her husband more celery, he has no staying power."

I frowned. "Put it through, will you, Maria?"

Suddenly I could hear traffic, and the slightly breathless voice of a man who was walking.

"Stone."

"Detective Stone, who was at the university before?"

"Yes, who am I speaking to?"

"My name is Am."

"Am?"

"Uh-huh, Am is for Americano, like the coffee."

I narrowed my eyes at Dehan, who was watching me with curious ones, and said, "I'm not really following you. Americano coffee?"

"The color, bro. My daddy had me with a black chick, called me Americano on account of the color of my skin."

"Oh, I see."

"We done with my name?"

"Yes, how can I help you, Am?"

"I was a student of Jose Robles. Me an' him had a special connection. He knew I was a genius. I figure maybe I can help you."

"You have information that can help us?"

"Maybe I have."

"Am, maybe isn't really good enough. Do you have information that can help the investigation or not?"

"Well, I don't know until I tell you, do I? You gotta decide that. Me an' him use to talk. We talked a lot. I told him 'bout my plans and my projects, an' the stuff I aim to do with my life, and he wanted to help me, you feel me? He was a good dude. I feel I owe him. I can tell you what we use to talk about, and then maybe there is somethin' in there that can help you."

I tried not to sigh. "Can you come in to the station, Am?"

He laughed. "No, man. I ain't goin' to no police station. I go in there, you ain't never gonna let me out again."

"Okay, give me your number and I'll call you when we..."

"No, man." He laughed again. "Don't give me that 'I'll call you' routine. You ain't never gonna call me. You think I'm as crazy as his lady. But I ain't crazy. You don't wanna talk to me, that's cool. I jus' wanna help the dude. You hear what I'm sayin' to you?"

"He's a little beyond helping, but I hear what you're saying. Where do you want to meet, Am?"

"You know where I live?"

I looked at Dehan, closed my eyes, and pinched the bridge of my nose. "No, Am, I don't know where you live."

"I'm gonna tell you. You know Hunts Point Avenue?"

"Yes."

"You know where it makes a kind of wishbone with Bryant Avenue?"

"Yes."

"Well *that's* where I live. Right there, dude. That's where I got me my *apartment*. It's new, you know?"

"And is that where you would like to meet?"

"Yeah, that would be cool. Do you think I need to be afraid, dude? 'Cause I am a witness."

I shook my head. "No, Am, I don't think you need to worry about that. Are you at home now?"

"I will be in about three minutes, maybe two. No, I think maybe three . . ."

"Stay there when you get home. We'll be right over."

I hung up and Dehan said, "Am?"

"It's a long story and not a very interesting one. Americano, milk with a dash of coffee. His father's idea."

"Nice."

I stood and grabbed my coat. "I think it's a waste of time, but he thinks he might have something. Let's go talk to him."

Am's apartment was the ground floor of an ugly, yellow brick house at the top of Bryant Avenue. By the time we got there, the afternoon was growing old and the temperature was turning from icy to glacial. A nasty gray light hung over everything, and a wind had started to pick up off the water that was damp and frigid and found its way into every nook and cranny of your clothing. I hammered on the door while Dehan stamped and billowed big clouds of condensation.

The door opened after a moment, and a big guy of about twenty-three or -four stood looking down at us. He must have been six-three in his bare feet. His complexion was dark, but he had blond hair and blue eyes.

"Are you Am?"

"I am," he said, apparently unaware that it could be amusing. "Are you the cops?"

"We are. This is Detective Dehan, and I am John Stone. Can we come in?"

"Yeah, man, you can come in. I'm making hot soup. Do you want some hot soup?"

"No, thank you." I waited. "But we *would* like to come in. It is very cold."

He grinned and stood back. "Yeah, sure, man!"

We stepped into a short, narrow hallway with a door on the left and a door at the end that stood open. Light filtered out, along with the smell of chicken soup. It smelled good. He scratched his head, looked embarrassed, and pointed at that door.

"I'm cooking . . . I'm making soup. I don't know if I should leave it on the stove . . ."

I smiled, wondering how many more nuts I was going to meet that day. "Why don't we all go into the kitchen? Then you can go ahead and cook, and we can talk there."

"Yeah, man, that's the plan." He walked ahead, muttering, ". . . man's got a plan."

The kitchen, like the hall, was small and narrow, but it was clean and well ordered. There was a table against the wall with two plastic chairs. A window over the sink looked out to a backyard, where inky silhouettes of winter trees stood stark against a darkening gray sky. Am went to his pot of soup, Dehan went and rested her backside against the sink, and I leaned against the door.

"What have you got to tell us about Jose Robles, Am?"

"He was takin' an interest in me, man. They was goin' to reject my application at the university, you know? But he told them, no way, man. He could see I had ideas. So he said he wanted me. Now he's dead."

We were all quiet for a moment while he stirred his soup. Eventually I sighed and said, "I am really sorry about that, Am, but I don't see how that can help us with our investigation . . ."

"I don't know, but I figure, if me an' him had a kind of special bond, you know what I'm sayin'? If you talk to me, then maybe you can, like, deduce why they wanted to kill him."

I glanced at Dehan. She closed her eyes and shook her head. I looked back at him and was going to thank him for his time and tell him it didn't work that way, but instead I heard myself asking him, "You live alone?"

"Yeah."

"Where are your parents?"

"Dad's in Colorado. Don't know where my mom is. She left when I was born." He looked at me and grinned. "She was colored, and he didn't like colored folk much. So he told her to git. Then he called me Americano 'cause he said I come out on the right side of brown."

I frowned, vaguely aware his voice was changing. "You grew up in Colorado?"

He took the pot off the heat and poured some soup into a mug. He glanced at Dehan. "You sure you don't want any?"

She smiled and nodded. "I'd love some actually. It smells great."

So he poured us a mug of soup each and said, "We can go to the living room. It's warm in there."

I glanced at my watch. "We can spare half an hour."

He had a fire burning in the grate and a couple of old, collapsed sofas that had been bolstered with blankets and cushions. He picked a corner opposite an old TV and smiled at us as we sat.

I sipped the soup. It was as good as it smelled. He watched me carefully and I nodded. "It's good. How long have you been in New York?"

"Since I turned sixteen. That's six years. It's why I talk funny. I kind of pick things up and mix it all together. Jose said it was a survival mechanism. I integrate to survive."

Dehan put her mug on the floor by her feet. "Your daddy teach you to make soup?"

"Uh-huh. He taught me everything. He taught me to survive."

"So what are the ideas that Jose was going to help you with?"

He stared at his soup for a while, then at the fire. "You heard about the Tesla. And there are dudes out in Texas makin' 'lectric motors from lithium-ion batteries. They'll go naught to sixty in one and a half seconds, man. And they will go two hundred MPH no problem. Problem those cars got though, is the battery loses its charge superfast. Fast as the car goes, that's how fast it loses its charge. Now, I have ideas, good ideas, about how you can stop that happenin', dude. And I told those ideas to Jose, Dr. Robles, and he said they was good ideas. An' that's why he wanted me in his class. I told him, I want to run my own company, dude, fitting kick-ass motors to classic chassis, you feel me? Gonna be wild and bitchin'. Tell you! He said, 'Yeah, you gonna do that, Am!' I said, 'You know I am!'" He sighed. "Now he's dead, I can't do that."

I shook my head. "He was helping you, Am, but it was always going to be you doing it. It may be more difficult now, but you can still do it. There must be other lecturers who can help you."

"Like Hays?" He laughed. "Hays is even more crazy than I am, man."

Dehan laughed. "Well, there you go! If he could do it, so can you!"

He laughed out loud. "Yeah, I like that. Right. If he can do it, so can I. Yeah, man."

I sat forward. "Am, did Jose ever talk to you about guns?"

"No way, dude. Me an' him did not agree on that score. I'm like my daddy. I believe in the Second Amendment, man. Ain't nobody gonna take my guns away from me, not while I's alive anyhow. But Jose was all about, if you give people guns, they will shoot each other. And I'm like, no, man. You give people guns and they will not shoot each other! You see me? I been around guns all my life, I never wanted to shoot nobody. Now, these boys around here? Guns pretty much illegal in New York, right? Well they can't wait to git their hands on a piece and shoot somebody!"

I laughed and shook my head. "You just can't decide whether you're a cowboy or a badass black dude, can you?"

"I told you, man. I talk weird."

"So Jose never asked you for a gun?"

"No way. And if he had, I would'a said no. I ain't givin' no gun to a dude like him."

"What about Agnes? She ever ask you for a gun?"

He hesitated. "I didn't know Agnes all that well. Never talked to her much. I seen her around with Jose, we never discussed nothing deep. She was real shy."

I nodded. "So was that something Jose specialized in? Lithium-ion batteries?"

"Yeah, man. He was lookin' at ways of replacing the liquid. That liquid can form dendrites, see? And they will kill the battery and maybe even catch fire, cause all kinds of problems. Now, you replace that liquid with another substance like glass, or other crystalline substances, or gel, it is gonna be, like, more stable and hold its charge much longer. Me and him, we use to have long conversations 'bout that, man. I had some cool ideas. He liked them. He told me I was a genius. I felt good about that."

"I bet you did. Did he ever discuss his personal life with you?"

He frowned. "Like what kind of thing?"

"His relationships with women, girlfriends, friends and family . . ."

His frown deepened. "No, he never talked about nothing like that. All he ever talked about was science, and the big revolution that was coming. He said men like me and him were gonna change the world. He said one day we would make a car called the Robles-Americano, and everybody would be drivin' the Robles-Americano. Charge it once a year, dude, two hundred and fifty miles per hour, naught to sixty in one second. Badass car, man."

I smiled. "A bit faster than my old Jaguar. Okay, Am, thanks for talking to us. And stay with the course, don't you go dropping out. We're going to be checking."

He nodded. "Was it helpful, what I told you?"

"I think it might be, yeah. Hang loose, dude."

He shook his head. "It sounds wrong when you say it."

I pointed at him. "It sounds wrong when you say it too!"

He laughed. "I know."

When we stepped outside, it was dark. The wind blowing in off the river now seemed to be driving invisible needles. We clambered in the car, and I put on the heating, pulled out onto Hunts Point Avenue, and headed for the expressway. After a couple of minutes Dehan said, "Can you please explain to me what just happened? Have we slipped into some kind of parallel universe where crazy is normal and we are the normal ones, who are crazy?"

I nodded. "Yes. That just about sums it up."

"Oh, okay, that's all right then." She was quiet for a moment longer and then said, "Because I thought I just met a mixed-race cowboy who tries to talk like Hollywood's idea of a black Bronx badass, and is in fact a genius who is going to revolutionize the world by creating a battery you only need to charge once a year."

"Yes."

"And I'll tell you one more thing. If there is one guy in the world who could have got Agnes her gun, it's him."

"Yup."

"Jose had this guy's dreams in the palm of his hand."

"Mm-hm."

"Stone, he was creating another dependency—just like he had Agnes, just like he had Hays, he was making Am emotionally dependent on him . . . That's what this son of a bitch did in life. He went through life making people dependent on him. That's how he got his kicks. He was a bully. A bully who created emotional dependency."

"That is what it looks like."

"And I can see how Agnes' jealousy could lead her to want to kill him, or Alicia Cobos, but what I cannot see, Stone, is why this kid, whose whole future depends on Jose Robles giving him a hand up, would provide Agnes with a gun! Why would he get Agnes a gun?"

"Why? Try rephrasing the question."

"Okay, okay, okay . . . What would make this kid give Agnes a gun . . . ?"

"That is more focused."

"He already said he wouldn't give a gun to Jose, so the only reason he would give one to Agnes is if she was going to shoot somebody he wanted dead . . ."

"Well, I'm not sure that's the only reason, but . . ."

"So what would make him want Jose dead?"

"That is a good question. And . . . ?"

"Jesus!" She stared at me. "If he was stealing Am's ideas. Why else would a guy like Jose Robles hang out with a kid like Am? And if he was using them in his research, they would become the property of the university and Am would be left out in the cold. That is one powerful motive for shooting somebody."

I nodded and sighed. "It surely is, partner. It surely is . . ." After a moment I added, "What I am not clear on, though, is why he would want to talk to us."

SIX

The traffic was heavy and slow-moving on the Bruckner Expressway, and the lights looked like boiled sweets in red and green and amber. My phone rang, and I handed it to Dehan. She answered the call and said, "Yeah, Dehan."

She listened for a bit and said to me, "It's Joe, from the lab. He has something he says we'll want to have a look at." She looked at her watch. "Let's go see him and call it a day." She didn't wait for me to answer. She said into the phone, "We're on our way, Joe. With this traffic, it's going to be half an hour at least."

She hung up and put the phone in my pocket. Then she said, "So, the question I am asking myself now is, does Am know where Agnes is?"

"You made up your mind about this?"

"No, I am exploring the idea. But frankly, Stone, so far it is the only idea that seems to have any chance of taking us anywhere."

"Okay, so talk me through it. How does this work?"

She shifted in her seat so she was facing me and stuck her gloved hands between her knees to keep them warm.

"Our starting point is that Jose Robles is an egomaniac, who gets a kick out of making weak people dependent on him. This is something he does for fun, for pleasure. It is the only way he knows how to have close, intimate relationships."

I glanced at her and frowned. "This is a theory; we have no evidence for this, except anecdotes from acquaintances."

"Don't interrupt. I know that. So, he gets into this relationship with Agnes. She is highly dependent and falls in love with him, or becomes obsessed with him, whichever. Maybe both. And the more dependent she becomes, the more cruel and dominant *he* becomes, to the point that he starts a relationship with Dr. Alicia Cobos and flaunts it to Agnes."

She went quiet. I glanced at her. "I know what's stalling you here. Jose and Ali started this relationship, but she was not dependent on him. In fact, your gut instinct is that she didn't even have sex with him. So you are wondering A, how does that relationship fit in with your theory? And B, what made her lie about having sex with him in the first place?"

She nodded. "Mm-hm . . ."

"Well, note the questions and come back to them later. Keep going, it's good."

"Okay, fine, he gets into this relationship as a way of torturing Agnes. What he doesn't realize is just how badly he is hurting her. The final straw comes when he tells her, get a cab, I am staying the night with Alicia. Then Agnes starts thinking about killing him."

"Okay, meanwhile . . ."

"Wait! Meanwhile, Dr. Jose Robles, whose field of specialization is lithium-ion batteries, has discovered a student who, though decidedly odd, is gifted in the field of science. And Dr. Jose Robles, while claiming to mentor him, actually starts to steal this kid's ideas and use them in his research. What he doesn't understand is that this kid is an evil mixture of Colorado cowboy and Bronx badass. This kid grew up around guns, and he knows a Sig Sauer P226 from a Glock 18 or a Desert Eagle. So when he realizes what Jose is doing, he approaches Agnes, discreetly, and plants the idea of revenge. He also facilitates the gun."

"Problems: How does he approach her without Jose noticing?

Also, how does he get close enough to her to plant such a radical idea and facilitate the gun? Bear in mind, with both of these questions, that she is with Jose all the time."

"At first, Sensei, but remember that after a time, he starts to get bored with her and enjoys dumping her. We have heard of two occasions, but how many more were there? Remember also that Hays told us he and Agnes used to prefer to eat their lunch in the student canteen. It is perfectly possible that Am approached her during her lunch hour and spoke to her."

"Yes, that is possible. We need to check it, talk to Hays again. I'll tell you what I am having the most trouble with."

"What?"

"Am as an evil genius. He may or may not be a scientific genius, but you would have to be very subtle, and very good at manipulating people, to persuade them to commit a murder and take the fall for it. I don't see Am in that role."

She was quiet for a long while, watching the cars ahead, with the amber light from the streetlamps washing over her face in a slow, steady rhythm.

Eventually we pulled off the expressway and turned onto Castle Hill Avenue and headed north toward Morris Park. Then she said suddenly, "I wonder how many Ams we've met. The name is a joke. First person of the verb 'to be.' One minute he's black Bronx, the next he's a Colorado redneck . . . 'I'm making soup, you want soup? I'm a bit weird and crazy, but I am also a loveable genius.' He got *us* to go to *him*, so he didn't have to step outside on a freezing-cold day, and we didn't even get his surname to check with the university."

I handed her my phone again. "Call him. Get his name."

I heard it ring a couple of times, then Dehan said, "Yo, Am, it's Detective Dehan. Listen, we need your name. We have to fill out a report, and we can't just call you Americano, right? What's your surname?" She glanced at me, then said, "Nielsen? And that's your permanent address on Bryant Avenue? Cool, Am, thanks for your help."

She hung up, then made another call.

"Good afternoon, this is Detective Carmen Dehan of the NYPD Forty-Third Precinct. We are investigating Dr. Jose Robles' murder, and I need to confirm that he had among his students one Americano Nielsen, also known as Am Nielsen . . . Okay, I'll hold." After a couple of minutes, she repeated the question, then: "He did? And he is now temporarily on Donald Hays' list of students? Thank you for your help."

She hung up and sat banging the edge of my phone on her thigh. "So, just for the sake of argument, humor me here: let's say Am is some kind of shape-shifter . . ."

"A what now?"

"You know what I mean, one of those people who can just become somebody else, like Meryl Streep. In *Death Becomes Her* she's this glamorous, sexy star, and then in *Bridges of Madison County* she is just like totally somebody else."

"Oh, okay, I get the idea."

"So just humor me, and imagine that Am is like that, he can take on any kind of personality he wants and be totally convincing. And by using that very skill, on a highly vulnerable, suggestible Agnes Shine, he convinces her to kill Jose. Now, the million-dollar question becomes, does he know where she went? I think that would have to be part of the plan. He would need to know where she was going, and where she was going to hide. I mean, she becomes a big risk and a loose end."

I nodded. "Yes, he would. He would need to know that. But I worry this theory is getting away from us. What is it actually founded on? The fact that his father is a Colorado redneck, and he is a little odd. There are a lot of suppositions here, Dehan."

She grunted, then sighed.

We were pulling into the grounds of the Van Etten Building. I said, "I'm not saying we shouldn't explore it, Little Grasshopper, but let's get a bit of evidence to build on first. Let's see what Joe has for us."

We huddled in our coats and crossed the freezing parking lot to the lobby, then rode the elevator up to the lab. We found Joe in his office, and he stood to greet us as we came in.

"Sit down, you want some coffee? It's cruel out there."

Dehan shook her head. "No, thanks. I just had some soup." I shook my head too, and he leafed through a stack of files till he found the one he was looking for.

"This was unexpected. Gutierrez had asked us to have a look at Jose Robles' phone, to see if we could get any idea of where Agnes Shine had fled to, and also why she killed him in the first place. So we had the tech guys doing an autopsy on the cell when we find a deleted app. We look into it, and we find he used to have Telegram."

Dehan raised her eyebrows. "No kidding."

"Exactly. Now, thousands of people have Telegram, there is nothing unusual about that. But it always raises a flag with us, because obviously it is the messenger app favored by terrorists and organized crime, the reason being it is so hard to decrypt, and the company is so uncooperative with the authorities. So, we had a look-see what we could retrieve. There was very little . . ." He opened the file and leafed through a few pages, then said, "Here, this is all we could get. He receives a message on the Thursday before he died that says, 'Maybe I should become your student,' to which he replies, 'I told you never to contact me on my phone!' The message was from somebody called . . ." He looked at us both in turn. "Mohamed. We are working on getting the phone number, but I thought you'd want to see this straightaway."

Dehan sighed loudly, pulled her hat off her head, and screwed it up into a ball. The static from the friction left small hairs standing up on her head like antennae.

"The fact that his name is Mohamed means nothing of itself."

Joe nodded. "Obviously. And the fact that his name was Mohamed and he was using Telegram is nothing more than slightly suggestive."

He smiled in a way that said that his uncle was the Sultan of Brunei and Alice in Wonderland was coming for tea on Sunday.

Dehan sighed again. "But add to that the fact that he deleted the app, and that the murder weapon was a pistol favored by pros . . . oh man!"

I said, "The number that sent the message will be a burner."

"In all probability, John. And the chances are he will have got rid of it by now. But if he hasn't, we might be able to get a fix on its location."

I looked at Dehan. She looked tired and cold. "Let's not jump the gun, Dehan. 'Maybe I should join your class.'" I looked at Joe. "It's a threat."

Joe nodded. "I agree. It certainly sounds like a threat."

Dehan had her lips pursed, like she was blowing a kiss at her hat. "To which his response is, don't contact me on my phone. The clear implication is that Jose has a secret he does not want revealed."

Joe nodded. "So far, that is sound, yes."

Dehan looked at him and then at me. "A secret that's called Mohamed and uses a Sig Sauer Tacops P226."

Joe leaned back in his chair and emitted a small, humorless laugh. "I'm just here to do the forensics, you guys have to put it all together and give it meaning, but don't forget that whoever was using that Sig put no less than eight rounds into Jose's body. He may have been using a pro's gun, but he wasn't shooting like a pro."

"He or she," I said. "Come on, Dehan. Let's get home and get some hot food inside us. Things will make more sense after a bottle of . . ."

I stopped, remembering the bottle on the table by Agnes' glass, the two dozen bottles in her kitchen and the two dozen more in Robles' kitchen, and the glass of whiskey by the sink.

For a fastidious man like Robles, the sequence was wrong.

They were both looking at me. Joe smiled. "A bottle of wine or a bottle of whiskey?"

I gave a small laugh that was more of a snort. "That's a good question, Joe. First a beer, or a martini if you want a cocktail, then the wine, and then a whiskey or a brandy to round it off. Isn't that the correct sequence?"

He looked at Dehan and laughed. "The man knows how to live. You have to hand it to him!"

Dehan was laughing and getting to her feet. "He does that! Why d'you think he married me? The man's got taste!"

"Can't argue with that!"

It was a short drive from the lab to the house. The streets were empty but for the occasional car that hissed by, casting amber light on the blacktop. The first Santas were beginning to scale the walls, balconies, and rooftops, and the first strings of winking lights were beginning to gild the lilies in the gardens of suburbia. I killed the engine of the Jag outside our house, and Dehan went ahead in her woolly hat and gloves to open the door.

Inside, as I closed the drapes and started to build the fire, she peeled off her layers of wool and went to the kitchen. I heard the fridge open and thud closed and pots and pans clatter, and the warmth of the growing flames washed over my hands and face. Then there was a pregnant silence from the kitchen. I stood, poured two generous Bushmills, and went to the breakfast bar with them.

She was standing, staring at a can of tomatoes. On the bar she had a pack of minced meat, an onion, some garlic, a red pepper, and a pack of spaghetti. I said, "It's a can of tomatoes. It has tomatoes in it. They grow them like that in Italy, in the cans, especially for making spaghetti and pizza."

She put down the can. I sipped my drink and went to look for a can opener, fearing dinner might be slow in coming if I didn't.

She said, "Who stands to lose the most if Jose Robles' research is successful?"

I set about opening the can. "That is a very wide question, Dehan. You'd need to be a bit more precise about what you mean."

I handed her a vegetable knife and an onion. She took them and frowned at me. "I mean, if everything that Am said is true. If they are on the verge of a revolution in lithium battery technology, and soon all forms of transport are going to be running on lithium-ion batteries. Who stands to lose the most?"

I ground some black pepper into the tomatoes and took the onion and the knife from her. "Peel the garlic, will you?" She picked up the garlic and followed me to the frying pan, where I peeled the onion and started cutting it into the pan. "Obviously the petroleum companies would be the worst hit. But, Dehan . . ."

"No, just humor me a moment, Stone. Where are the most powerful petroleum interests in the world?"

I took the garlic from her fingers and started peeling it. "Slice the red pepper for me. Saudi, Egypt, the UAE, Jordan, Iraq . . . all of them. I know where you're going with this . . ."

She went and came back waving a red pepper at me. "Don't talk, just answer the question. Now, obviously, if you are heavily invested in oil, you can't go around murdering every scientist who comes up with an alternative energy source. But what you can do is try and take possession of that technology."

I took the pepper from her and said, "Olive oil, and salt." I started chopping the pepper. "Yes, that is true. But how do you get from there to . . ."

"I said don't talk. Now, suppose a Middle Eastern government got to hear about Dr. Jose Robles' research, and they approached him to buy him out . . ."

I took the olive oil from her hands and poured it into the pan, with the onion, the garlic, and the red pepper, then turned on the heat. She had gone quiet. I took the salt and sprinkled it in. The pan started to sizzle. I stirred it with a wooden spoon.

"Hand me the meat and open the wine."

She brought over the pack of meat in one hand and the bottle in the other. As she started peeling off the lead from the bottle, she sighed and shook her head. "Whichever way you look at it, there is always something that doesn't fit."

I nodded. "I keep wondering about that threat: to join his class."

She screwed the corkscrew in, stuck the bottle between her knees, and pulled. The cork popped. She carried the bottle away and put it on the table. Then she came back and leaned her cheek on my shoulder, watching the onions brown. "Wanting to own or control his research is a motive for blackmail, even torture, but it's not a motive for murder."

I dumped the meat into the hot oil and started breaking it up. "Yup. But whoever shot him really wanted him dead."

"That much is clear." She went and started filling a pan with water. "But I'll tell you what else is clear: we need to start looking at his research. Because it either has everything to do with his murder, or it has nothing to do with it."

SEVEN

Next day, we were knocking at the deputy inspector's door at eight thirty a.m. He made a muffled noise from within, which we took to mean "enter" and opened the door. He had his face in a large paper cup of coffee, which explained the muffled noise, and one arm out of his coat.

"Good morning, Detectives. How can I help you?"

Dehan relieved him of his coffee and helped him off with his coat while I sat and said, "We need a court order to see Jose Robles' research, sir."

He frowned, then smiled as he thanked Dehan, and returned to frowning as he sat behind his desk. "Clearly you think there is a connection between his murder and his research, and that's why you want the court order, but if I recall correctly it looked as though his colleague . . . um . . ."

"Agnes Shine."

"Exactly, had shot him out of jealousy, or something like that."

Dehan was wearing the expressionless expression she wore when people got on her nerves. Now she used it to say, "But the case was given to us, sir, because the ADA didn't like that explanation."

He grunted. "So what makes you think it has something to do with his research?"

I'd been rehearsing it in my mind all the way there that morning, and I still couldn't nail it. I looked at Dehan and she shook her head. "There is no single thing, sir," she said. "It's a number of small things that, when you take them together, suggest very strongly that ADA Varu . . . that the assistant district attorney may be right, and the murder has more to do with Robles' research than his love life."

The inspector smiled at her. "That's your introduction, Detective, now what are your reasons?"

She looked at me, and I took a deep breath.

"Let's start with the gun, sir. It was a Sig Sauer Tacops P226. That is a professional's choice of gun. It is expensive and not the sort of thing you buy just for home defense. It is something you would use for a hit, or for an execution, or if you were being shipped out to Afghanistan, but not if you just wanted a gun around to make you feel safe."

He flopped back in his chair. "There could be any number of explanations . . ."

"Bear with me, sir. As Dehan said, it's an accumulation of things. Then there is the fact that all those who knew Robles and Agnes are adamant that neither of them would own a gun, far less spend the kind of money you're going to spend on a Sig. So already we are seeing the as yet unexplained presence of an unregistered, professional's choice of handgun at the scene of the murder.

"Next, and still on the subject of the gun, there is no sign in her financial records that she made an outlay of a thousand bucks in the weeks leading up to the murder; plus, it is hard to imagine Agnes Shine would have any idea in the first place of where to find an unregistered weapon. So the deeper we go, the more we have to wonder how *that particular* gun comes to be at the scene of the murder."

He sighed. "I am far from convinced, John. What else have you got?"

"Well, sir, on top of the unexplained presence of the gun, there is no indication that Jose and Agnes were in any way involved with each other except as friends. They spent a lot of time together, he was cruel and unkind to her at times, but so far we have no reason at all to believe that they were lovers. I, personally, am still struggling to see what her motive was.

"Finally, we have reason to believe, from testimony given by one of his students, that he was engaged in some radical research into lithium-ion batteries that could be worth a fortune. *That* could provide a serious motive for murder, and we have forensic evidence that he was in secret communication with somebody called Mohamed. So there is an at least even chance that the motive for the murder stemmed from his research, rather than his sex life."

He grunted and sipped his coffee. "You know I like to give you guys every assistance I can, John. But no judge in New York is going to sign off on a request like that, where highly sensitive research is concerned. I agree you have grounds for suspicion, but you have no grounds whatsoever to *believe* that his research is behind the motive. That is a very different proposition."

Dehan sighed. "We need to see that research, sir."

"He was at University College New York, wasn't he?"

"Yes, sir."

"Then, at this stage, the best thing you can do is go and talk to his head of department, explain your concerns, and ask to see his research. Point out it will not become public property, we are prepared to sign a nondisclosure agreement, and that the safety of other researchers may be at risk. That is the best you can do at this stage."

We thanked him, and on the way down the stairs, I pulled out my cell and called Patricia Meigh. When she answered, I could hear children in the background.

"Detective Stone, how can I help you?"

"In a big way, I hope. We have reason to believe Dr. Robles' murder may have been related to his work, and not to his private life."

"That is absurd."

I stopped on the stairs. Dehan turned to watch me. I suppressed a pellet of anger in my belly and said, "With all due respect, Dr. Meigh, how would you know that?"

The momentary silence said she'd been taken aback. Then she said, "Well, I mean, how could it be?"

"That is a question, and a very good one. But what you made before was a statement of fact and an unfounded one. So with your permission, I am going to go with the question. Our investigation has turned up several inconsistencies which suggest it is possible Agnes Shine did not kill Dr. Robles, but that his murder may have been related to his research. If we are right, then other people on your team could be at risk."

"I see . . ."

"Now we can apply for a judicial order, but then you'll have to get your lawyers involved, it will be costly and slow, and during that time somebody else could get hurt . . ."

She cut me short. "Look, Detective, there is no need for all that. Just give me half an hour and I'll get back to you."

We returned to our desks and Dehan lowered herself into her chair. Outside it had started drizzling and the tops of the naked branches across the road were bouncing gently in the desultory, wet wind. It occurred to me it was almost Christmas. I smiled down at Dehan.

"We have to get the tree."

She nodded. "Tonight."

Behind me, Mo at his desk said, "Hey, you know, this year you ain't allowed to say Merry Christmas, in case it offends the GBL . . . whatever, bacon, lettuce, and tomato brigade, on account of Christians being homophobic. Now we gotta say a Gay Christmas and a Rainbow New Year. Seriously. I read it in the paper. If you don't believe me, look in the *Post*. I got it right here."

Dehan put her boots up on the desk. "They have words in that? I thought it was just pictures."

Mo grinned. "Hey, you know why Jesus wasn't born in Vegas?"

"I know you're going to tell me."

"They couldn't find three wise men and a virgin!" He laughed noisily. "That's good. Three wise men and a virgin. I like that. Like you're gonna find three wise men and a virgin in Vegas! Right!"

He turned back to his desk, shaking his head and laughing. My phone rang.

"Stone."

"Morning, Stone. Joe. Okay, it's piecemeal, but I'm giving you what I've got. We took all the bedding from Dr. Shine's house and Dr. Robles' house. We kept it all in three separate piles: on the bed, in the dirty washing, and clean and in storage, so that they would not contaminate each other."

"Good."

"Now, as a first step, we examined each piece of bedding to see if they did in fact have any latent fluids. We examined them thoroughly."

"And?"

"They didn't."

"Could they have been washed out?"

"No, recoverable semen stains will resist time and the washing machine, John. There was not a trace on any of the sheets. I'd be prepared to swear he never had sex in his own bed. Nobody had sex in his bed. And the same goes for her. They seem to have been celibate, at least in their own beds."

I frowned down at Dehan, then asked, "What about the glasses?"

"Working on it."

"Thanks, Joe. I appreciate it."

I hung up and sat. "There was no sexual relationship between them, Dehan. The sheets were clean. Not a trace of semen on his or hers."

"All the damn forensic evidence we have is negative. It all shows what didn't happen and who didn't do it."

"We need to find this Mohamed guy. We need to know what he wanted from Jose, and why it was a threat for Jose to have Mohamed in his class." I leaned back in my chair. "Why do I keep getting the feeling we need to talk to Am again?"

Dehan shrugged. "If Dr. Meigh won't play ball, maybe he can give us a better insight into the research they were doing."

"Yeah, maybe. Let's see what Meigh gives us." I drummed my fingers on the desk for a bit. "You know one of the things that's eating me? How did Jose find out about Am? He said they didn't want to accept him on the course, but Jose recognized his genius. How? How did he even know he existed?"

"Through his application."

I made a QED face and said, "If his conversation is anything to go by, his application form wouldn't exactly have screamed IQ a hundred and sixty. He may be brilliant when it comes to electronics and engineering, Dehan, but when it comes to communication . . ."

She narrowed her eyes. "What are you driving at?"

"I don't know, but I can smell something. There's Mohamed, 'Maybe I should join your class,' and Jose replying, 'I told you never to contact me on my phone!' And then he deletes Telegram. So what did he have it for in the first place? And then there's Am, coming to Jose's notice *before* he joined his class. Before he was even admitted to the university."

I studied Dehan's face for a while and she studied mine back. She said, "It's odd, isn't it? 'I told you never to contact me on the phone.' Not 'this phone,' but 'the phone.' So, how else would he contact him?"

"Email and Facebook, but they are not as secure as Telegram."

She nodded then said, "But he obviously didn't know that, which is telling us something."

"It's telling us he was not steeped in spook lore." I sat forward with my elbows on the desk and rubbed my face with my palms. "If you were selling industrial secrets to the Saudis, and they advised you to install Telegram so they could communicate with you, would you then tell them *not* to contact you on your phone, and delete the app?"

"Doesn't make a lot of sense, does it?"

"We are going round and round the mulberry bush."

My phone rang.

"Stone."

"I thought they only did that in the movies, Detective. This is Dr. Meigh. I have spoken to the Great and the Good at the university and they are willing to let you have sight of the research he had conducted so far. Obviously most of it will mean nothing to you, but he had extensive explanations and summaries that he had written in longhand which describe the work in layman's terms."

"That is good news. Thank you."

"Now, there are conditions."

"I imagined there would be."

"We would like you to read the notes here, at my house. Nothing is to leave the room where you read it. You are not to photograph or record any part of the research, and we would require you to sign a nondisclosure agreement that, unless the research becomes material to a criminal investigation or a criminal trial, the NYPD, and you personally, will become liable to compensate the university in substantial damages if you disclose any of the contents of the research. And I do mean substantial."

"That sounds very reasonable. Send over the agreement and I'll get the inspector to sign it."

"And you and your partner, Detective Stone."

"And me and my partner, Dr. Meigh."

"I'm sending it now. As soon as I receive the signed copy, you can come over. I'm at Port Washington for the next few days. Number fifty-five, Joel Place."

The agreement arrived five minutes later by secure electronic messenger. We took it up to the inspector and scrutinized it. It was short and to the point, pretty much what she had said to me on the phone.

"I should send this to the legal department." He said it running his fingers through his hair.

Dehan suppressed a sigh. "With all due respect, sir, that would kind of defeat the purpose. Once the lawyers get involved, it could delay the investigation by weeks. If we don't find anything, it makes no odds. If we do, and it becomes relevant to the investigation, it's in black and white. We can use it. Then we can bring in the lawyers."

I said, "It's two paragraphs. Send it to ADA Varoufakis. See what he thinks."

He tapped at his keyboard, then made the call.

"Costas? This is John Newman . . . Good, I'm fine. Listen, I just sent you something on the Jose Robles case . . . Yes, I have my best team on it. You got an email from me?" He was quiet for a while. Then he said, "You happy with that?"

He was quiet again, watching us. Then he said, "I'll pass it on. They'll be in touch."

He hung up and stared at the rim of his desk for a moment.

"He considers it is fine. He would like us all to get together for a talk when you have reviewed Robles' research."

Dehan spoke my own thoughts. "What is his interest in this case, sir?"

"I have no idea, Carmen. But I am becoming as curious as you are. I am curious about his interest, and I am very curious as to why Dr. Meigh has agreed to your having sight of the research."

Dehan frowned. "Because she agrees there is a threat to her other researchers?"

He shook his head. "It doesn't work that way, Carmen. If his research was so sensitive that it got him killed, the university would deny everything vehemently, close ranks, and triple their private security. The research conducted by the major universities is worth billions of dollars; it can be highly classified material, attract massive government funding, and in those cases is guarded by ex–Navy SEALs who work in the private sector. But instead of closing ranks and denying everything, she is inviting you to her house and opening the books."

Dehan raised an eyebrow. "Then she has nothing to hide."

"Then why the big show? Why the nonsense about not leaving the room, not making copies or photographs, the nondisclosure agreement? And why does Costas want a meeting afterwards?" He looked up at me. "This case has too many angles, John. What is it all about?"

I called Patricia Meigh.

"Detective, all in order?"

"It's agreed and signed. Have you received it?"

She was quiet a moment, then said, "I have. Thank you."

"We are on our way. We'll see you within the hour." I hung up. "Let's go find out."

EIGHT

It was a forty-minute drive under heavy skies, sagging and pregnant with rain, sleet, and snow. The East River looked as though it was congealing into ice, and the trees we saw along the Cross Island Parkway looked like naked zombies standing in line in a freezer. After Lake Success there were more evergreens and pines, but they did little to alleviate the gloom.

Dehan sat silent for the first twenty minutes, wrapped once again in her woolen hat, gloves, and scarf, with her hands tucked between her knees. But as we slowed and started winding our way toward Manhasset, she said suddenly, "If this is what it's starting to look like, we'll have to hand it over to the Feds."

I nodded. "If it is what it's starting to look like, but the truth is, Dehan, it could look like a lot of things. Mohamed and a Sig Sauer make it look like Saudi industrial spies; Agnes and eight bullet holes in Robles' chest make it look like frustrated love and sex. Am and his weird voices make it look like the Mad Hatter's tea party. Let's reserve judgment and see what it looks like after Dr. Meigh shows us Robles' research notes."

She glanced at me, then looked out at the frozen landscape. "You think Varoufakis has information he's holding back from us?"

"Yup. It makes no sense his sending us on this investigation unless he knows something he isn't telling us."

"Something about Jose? About Agnes? Or about the research?"

I sat chewing my lip for a while as we cruised through Plandome Heights, with its genteel manor houses concealed behind a discreet overabundance of foliage. "Something," I said, "about who Mohamed is, and how Dr. Jose Robles met Am."

She knitted her brows under her soft wool hat. "Seriously? You think he knows about that?"

"I'd be very surprised if he didn't."

Ten minutes later, we pulled into Patricia Meigh's driveway and parked beside a Jaguar that was fifty-four years younger than mine, and had a tenth of the style and the class. Dehan looked at my expression, then at the car, and laughed a pretty laugh with a red nose and red cheeks. "These upstarts," she said, and climbed out.

Dr. Meigh opened the door herself. Behind her we could hear voices: a small group of people laughing and chatting. She offered us the smile that good form required of her but left us in no doubt that we were intruding, and not welcome.

"Detectives, please come in." We stepped into a spacious, elegant hall. She didn't offer to take our coats but turned and started walking away, past the door to the drawing room, where the voices were coming from, and speaking over her shoulder as she went. "I have put you in the dining room. We shan't be using it until this evening. I imagine you'll be finished by then?"

We followed her down a dark, wood-paneled corridor to a large, wood-paneled dining room. There was, in the middle of the floor, a highly polished mahogany dining table with twelve chairs about it, and above it a crystal chandelier. Two tall sash windows allowed dull, gray light in from the gardens and the driveway outside. A dull amber light was added to that when she snapped on a switch by the door.

On the table there were two cardboard boxes. She closed the door and moved to them.

"This is what there is. Most of it is equations, which, unless one of you is an accomplished physicist or mathematician, will not mean much to you. However, quite a lot of it is, as I said to you on the phone, his theories and explanations of the equations. From them you will at least get an idea of what he was doing, though I am honestly not sure how that will help you."

I held her eye a moment. "Dr. Meigh, you said when we spoke to you in your office that Dr. Robles and Dr. Shine were involved. I believe your exact words were that they were not so much involved *with* each other as *in* each other."

"Yes, that's true."

"Detective Gutierrez's assumption, and ours to begin with, was that this involvement provided the motive for the murder."

"That would seem to make sense."

I nodded and paused. "But actually, the deeper we dig, the less evidence we find that they were in any kind of relationship. They seem to have been little more than close friends."

She looked surprised. "Well, of course, I didn't know them socially . . ."

Dehan had pulled off her hat and gloves and the static from the wool was making some of her hairs stand up and wave around again. She started to remove her coat and said, "In fact, the person he seems to have had a closer, sexual relationship with is Dr. Cobos."

She arched a withering eyebrow. "Really? Well, as I say, there is no accounting for taste."

I smiled. "You don't approve?"

She shook her head. "It is hardly for me to approve or disapprove. They are probably ideal for each other. They can celebrate their great nation together." I drew breath, but she interrupted me. "They have produced world-class painters and musicians, but never a world-class scientist or a world-class philosopher. That tells you something about their culture, I suppose."

I forced myself to hold the smile. "Are you able to enlighten us any more on their relationship, Dr. Meigh?"

"I'm afraid not. It was generally accepted among the staff that Jose and Agnes were, so to speak, an item. People spoke of 'Jose and Agnes' as a unit. People used to ask, 'What does she see in him?' So you see, they were perceived as a couple. What actually went on with them in private . . ." She shrugged.

"Sure." I nodded a couple of times and pursed my lips at the floor. As she was about to leave, I said, "What can you tell me about Am Nielsen?"

She stopped dead. "Am Nielsen? Nothing. Who is he?"

"One of Dr. Robles' students."

She shook her head again. "I'm sorry, I don't know him, and I really must get back to my family; we have a luncheon and then we are busy packing." A little warmth trickled back into her face. "We always spend Christmas in Maine. If you would like tea or coffee, just ring the bell and somebody will come." She hesitated, and the frost returned to her eyes. "You can let yourselves out when you are finished. I trust you not to remove any of the notes."

"That's very kind of you, Dr. Meigh."

She gave a smile that matched her eyes and left, closing the door behind her. Dehan opened the boxes and looked inside. "We have been quarantined, in case we infect her family with vulgarity and commonness."

I rang the bell, took off my coat, and dragged one of the boxes to the end of the table. There I pulled everything out and sat to examine it. It was mainly spiral-bound notebooks, though there were a few documents consisting of typewritten sheets of A4, stapled together, and the odd slip of paper with handwritten scrawls on it.

The door opened, and a young woman in a blue uniform with a white apron stepped in and smiled at us. I smiled back.

"Would you bring us a pot of coffee, please? Oh, and a plate of cheese and ham sandwiches. Thank you."

"Of course, sir." She bobbed and left.

Dehan was reading and didn't look up, but she smiled and said, "You don't know if you don't ask, right?"

"That's what I thought."

Dr. Meigh had been right. The bulk of what was in the notebooks was incomprehensible. Even where words were used, they didn't seem to make any kind of ordinary sense: *Consequently energy density denotes volume necessary to store X energy (Wh/Liter)...*

Or: *... power density as power/area shd b correlated to area available on the electrodes leading to W/cm².*

I sighed and looked over at Dehan. She seemed to be engrossed. I read aloud: "Internal resistance and V0 are derived from slop and y-intercept respectively. Did you know that?"

She didn't look at me. "Really? Mo must have a lot of internal resistance then. I don't know how much we are going to learn from this, Sensei. We may as well be reading ancient Greek."

"I think we are."

There was a knock at the door and the maid came in with a large tray. She placed it on the table and unloaded it. On an impulse I said, "Did you make the sandwiches yourself?"

"I did, sir. I wasn't sure if you'd like mustard and pickle, so I brought them along separately."

I smiled. "That's very thoughtful. Agnes said you make the best sandwiches."

She looked startled, but her face lit up. "She did? That's so kind of her. That was a long time ago. Back in the early fall! We hardly ever make sandwiches, ordinarily."

"Well, she still remembers them."

"That's so kind of her. Thank you, sir."

She gave a little curtsey, backed out of the room, and closed the door. I sat staring at the space where she had stood. I heard Dehan's voice.

"You're a sly old fox, Stone."

"Sandwiches." I turned to look at her. "As she said, not a thing

Dr. Meigh would normally eat, especially with doctor guests. It might have been afternoon tea, or, in early fall, a picnic. What do you think?"

"I think you should focus on the research and stop chatting up the staff."

I logged the fact under "curious" and went back to reading the illegible and trying to understand the incomprehensible. The enterprise was a predictable failure, until I came to two notebooks which had "Analysis" written on the front cover.

It took an hour, but I worked my way steadily through half a plate of sandwiches, half a pot of coffee, and a detailed discussion comparing various types of battery. It concluded that lithium-ion batteries (Li-ion or LIBs) were the ones with the highest potential for future development and, in a second notebook, detailed all the weaknesses of the LIB and where they needed to be improved. Then, quite suddenly, the discussion stopped.

I tossed the two notebooks in front of Dehan. "They're worth reading. You come across anything on how the LIB can be improved?"

"Probably, but if I did it was incomprehensible to me."

"Nothing in plain English?"

"No, but I found a few emails in plain Spanish."

"Really?"

She made a face. "Nothing much, to some guy called Paco Robles. Maybe his brother. Mostly he's complaining about the States, people aren't friendly, food is crap, yadda yadda, but here he says there is this girl who hangs around with him all the time. 'She's a pain in the ass, but she and her friend who is called like the duck, Donald, adore me, they go everywhere with me, but most Saturday nights I go out alone to a club in Chelsea, at 250 West Twenty-Sixth Street, after my colleague, *la colega*'—it's like, 'the chick'—'is in bed. Then I have a great time picking up chicks.'" She looked up at me. "Explains why his sheets are clean. He's been busy messing up somebody else's."

"This stuff must have been gathered up in a hurry."

"Yeah. Anyway, we came looking for industrial espionage evidence and found more crime of passion evidence."

I gave a smile that was rueful. "Looks like I'm going to have to take you dancing, Detective Dehan. It will be almost like old times."

"I can't wait." She didn't sound like she meant it.

At twelve thirty, we heard the party leave the house. From snatches of their conversation, I gathered they were going to La Piccola Liguria for a family luncheon.

I stood and went to the window. Across the lawn I could see the driveway. There was a couple with two kids of about ten and twelve getting into the Jaguar. Beyond them, I could see a white Audi reversing out of a garage. There was a man with his back to me. He seemed to be in his late forties, with short, black hair and a dapper suit. The Audi stopped and Meigh got out. They kissed, and she handed him the keys. He said something to her, they both laughed, and she ran into the house while he got behind the wheel. A moment later, she came out again, wearing a scarf. She got in next to him and they drove away, to the Piccola Liguria. A family. A happy family approaching Christmas.

After that, we worked on for another three hours, and at the end of it we had found nothing of interest, other than his email to his brother. Dehan photographed it on her cell, on the grounds that it was not research and was therefore not covered by the confidentiality agreement, and I stood to get my coat. I also pressed the bell to call the maid.

She entered as we were putting the notebooks back in the boxes. I smiled at her.

"What's your name?"

"Cynthia, sir."

"Cynthia, I am going to tell Dr. Meigh that you were extremely helpful, and very charming with it." She blushed and bobbed and thanked me very much. I gave what I hoped was a paternal smile and said, "You know Dr. Shine has gone missing."

"Yes, sir, but I don't really know anything about it."

"You probably know more than you realize. You know that Dr. Meigh, Detective Dehan, and I are trying to clear her name. We feel that she has been wrongly accused of the murder of Dr. Robles."

I could feel Dehan's eyes burning into the back of my head, but I ignored her. Cynthia's eyes were wide. I said, "I had hoped to have a chat with Patricia—with Dr. Meigh—before leaving, but it seems I've missed her. So maybe you can help me a little more before we go."

"I'd be glad to, Detective, if I can . . ."

"You see, it's essential we find Agnes soon, before she does anything . . ." I let the words hang there a moment until Cynthia nodded once, slowly. "So, maybe you can tell me when was the last time that she visited Dr. Meigh?"

She frowned hard. "Well, it's hard to say, exactly. You see, she used to come over most Saturdays, sometimes Friday, and the last Saturday she was here was the Saturday before she . . ." She hesitated a moment, then concluded, "Before she went away . . ."

"You see? That is so helpful. Obviously she'd stay till Sunday, they'd have a picnic . . ." I laughed. "All the usual stuff."

She was beginning to look troubled, like she knew she was being pumped and the doctor would be mad at her for talking to me. She nodded. "Yes, she always spent the weekend here."

I slipped her ten bucks and my card and winked at her. "You have been very helpful, Cynthia. If you think of anything at all, however small, which you think might help us to find Dr. Shine before she does anything foolish, you give me a call, anytime, night or day. Got it?"

She nodded, and we left.

In the car once again, Dehan looking more like a wool elf than a wood elf, we backed out onto the road and started the slow, freezing drive back toward the Bronx. She crossed her arms and her ankles and stuck out her bottom lip in thought.

"Well," she said, "that was surprising."

"We came looking for one thing, and we found three different things instead."

She looked at me from under her eyebrows. "Three?"

"Number three, I grant you, was a negative find, but, one." I held up my thumb. "We found that Dr. Jose Robles did in fact have a sex life." I held up my index finger. "Two, we found that he pursued it while Agnes was country housing on the weekends with her exalted friend Patricia Meigh; and, *and*, no less important than those two interesting facts, Dehan." I held up my middle finger. "We found that there was *absolutely nothing* remarkable about Dr. Robles' research. In fact, there was a bit of that research missing."

She smirked a little smugly. "We also found something else. I said 'three' like that because I counted four things."

"Four?"

"We also found that Dr. Meigh lied to us when she said she was not that close to Agnes. She was close enough that they got together every weekend to go sailing and have picnics."

I nodded. "Indeed, Little Grasshopper, indeed, we found that too. And that is very important."

"You think she's hiding Agnes?"

"It's possible, isn't it?"

"You think Cynthia will come through?"

"No. I did my best, but I don't think so."

"Oh, you did better than that. Poor kid's knees were knocking with the postpubescent hormonal riot that you unleashed inside her."

"Where do you learn to say such horrible things, Dehan?"

"From reading your books."

"So, what have we got?"

"May I?"

"Please do."

"Jose and Agnes got into this very intense relationship based on emotional dependency. He was dominant and she was subservient. The most important aspect of this difference was that she depended entirely on him, whereas he had this insatiable need to have lots of people dependent on him. That need drove him to seek out other people, like Hays and possibly Am Nielsen."

"Okay."

"Now, the thing is, their relationship is completely platonic. We don't know if it's him or her or both of them who don't want it, but we do know it ain't happening. We also know that he may be hitting the sack with Alicia Cobos and that Saturday nights he is going to a club where he has lots of fun. Does Alicia go with him? We don't know."

"We'll have to ask."

"Now, my theory: Agnes wants their relationship to progress to the next level. She wants a full-blown romantic relationship with him. But he only gets turned on by women who are *not* subservient." She held up a woolen hand. "Don't interrupt. He enjoys the power of dominating, but he only gets horny with women who *don't* need him. That's why he can't with Agnes, but he can with Ali and he can with the hookers—nobody is less emotionally dependent than a hooker, right?"

"Right. You have changed your mind about Alicia?"

"Jury's out. Anyway, Agnes gets to hear about his Saturday night capers, probably from Alicia. She calls him to her house, confronts him with it, and he follows their usual routine and humiliates her. But this time, the pain of rejection is too much, and she shoots him. The moment she realizes what she has done, she panics, jumps in her car, and drives to her friend Patricia, who hides her and her car." She turned and looked back over her shoulder at the receding road. "She is probably in that house right now."

I thought about it for a while, trying to visualize her in some kind of ménage à trois with Meigh's husband. It didn't really work.

"Questions: What about the gun, what about the research, and what about Assistant DA Costas Varoufakis?"

NINE

Instead of turning right toward the Bronx, I continued straight on through Queens and Brooklyn toward Manhattan. Dehan was saying, "The gun we already said might have any number of explanations. The research, she is just trying to fob us off because they are secretive about their products. It's natural. As for the ADA, I don't know, maybe he saw the same things we saw and thought it needed a deeper look than Gutierrez was giving it."

I nodded like I was listening and agreeing, but I wasn't. I said, "Call Hays, will you? Ask him if Am is there. Don't tell him we're on our way. Just ask."

She put it on speaker. It rang a couple of times, then Hays' voice said, "Yes?"

"Dr. Hays, this is Detective Dehan. You remember we spoke yesterday."

"Well, of course I remember. I would have to have some kind of very serious condition . . ."

I interrupted him. "Dr. Hays, we are phoning to ask about one of your students, Am Nielsen. Is he there today?"

"Yes, he was in class today. He's in all day."

On an impulse I asked him, "What kind of student is he, Dr. Hays?"

"I have only had him a very short time, but I know Jose thought very highly of him, and from what I have seen of his work, I would say he is above average."

"Would you describe him as eccentric?"

"No. Not any more than most science students at this level. You don't have to be insane to be a scientist, Detective, but it helps." There was an odd noise, as though he was suffocating, and I realized he was laughing.

"That's funny, Dr. Hays. I'll have to remember it."

"I hope you do. Your recall expectations seem to be quite low, if your partner is anything to go by."

"Dr. Hays, I have one more question before you go. Who has replaced Dr. Robles on the research program?"

"Nobody as yet."

"Right, okay, thank you."

We arrived at the university twenty minutes later. It was already getting dark. As we entered the lobby, I noticed a security guard. He was in his fifties, tall and wiry, and strongly built. He saw me looking at him and approached. He had a badge on his pocket with the legend VMS.

"Can I help you?"

I showed him my badge. "Detective Stone. We're looking for Am Nielsen."

He smiled. "There're an awful lot of students here, Detective . . ."

"This guy is a joker, six-three, athletic, imitates accents . . ."

He gave a lopsided smile and pointed toward the cafeteria. "That him?"

"That's him. Thanks."

He was sitting at a table with half a dozen other students. A couple of them were playing chess. There was a lot of talking and a lot of laughing, so they didn't notice us approaching till we were almost upon them. But I did notice that Am was getting most of the laughs, poking fun at the guy whose move it was.

"Mate in six, dude! No! Are you crazy? Not the bishop! Okay! Good move! If you want to lose your queen, do that!"

We stood, one on either side of him, and Dehan said, "Hello, Mr. Nielsen."

He jumped and turned, then gaped, and for a long moment he seemed only to be able to blink at her. Then he turned and looked at me. Finally, he said, "Detectives . . ."

I turned to the rest of the table. They were frowning. "Mind if we borrow your joker for a bit?"

Dehan winked at him. "Let's go for a walk. You feel me, dude?"

We walked him out to the lobby. The VMS guard had gone. We found a nest of chairs and sat. He drew breath, but I raised a hand. "Let's get the ground rules set first. Right now we are going to prosecute you for obstruction of justice. That will end your career as an engineer, and you will probably do time. Tell me another lie and you will be looking at accessory to murder." He went pale. "Now, start talking and convince me not to prosecute you. Here's a hint. Do that by telling me the truth."

"About what?"

Dehan shook her head, squinting at him. "How about you start by explaining why the stupid act."

He took a breath, then sighed and shrugged. "I'm a clown. It's compulsive. I get with people and I start clowning. When you came to see me, I just got caught up in the act."

"That's bullshit."

"No, man, it's not."

I sighed. "Come on, Am. You called me on the phone, remember? Why the hell did you call me? You have a university full of students you can clown with. You seriously expect us to believe that you called two cops on a homicide investigation just because you felt like clowning?"

"No, no, no, of course not. I called you because we'd all heard that Dr. Shine was a suspect in Dr. Robles' murder. It was eating at me. We all knew he treated her like shit, but she's a really sweet woman and there was no way she shot him. I was sure his death had something to do with his research. I can't tell you why. It was just a hunch. I knew if I called and said, 'I'm Dr. Robles' student and I think he was murdered for his research, but I have no evidence,' you'd laugh at me and send me on my way."

"So you came up with *that*! You couldn't think of anything more elaborate?"

"No, man. I didn't come up with it; I called, and when you answered, all kind of 'Stone!' I started playing a part, and before I knew it . . ."

"So how much of it was true?"

"Pretty much all of it. It's just, the way I told it was kind of elaborate."

"Your dad in Colorado, your name . . ."

"Yeah, man. Maybe not quite so dramatic as I made it sound, but it's all true."

Dehan pulled off her hat. "You said Robles intervened for you to be admitted . . ."

"No, I was admitted to the university in the ordinary way. But I got a reputation for being a clown. I have a bad habit of mimicking the teachers in tutorials and shit. That's not helpful in a serious institution like this one, however high your IQ is. So when I applied to assist on Dr. Meigh's research program, initially they said no, but Robles intervened and got me on."

"So you already had a good relationship with him."

"Yeah, very good."

I cleared my throat and frowned. "The whole thing about the Robles-Americano electric engine . . . ?"

He nodded. "We talked about that."

"Okay, so here's the thing, I have just come from looking at his research and there is absolutely nothing exceptional about it at all. All he does is review existing technology and discuss how it can be improved. But there is nothing, *nothing*, in the way of solid proposals."

"How could you possibly have seen . . ."

"Dr. Meigh gave us access."

He stared at me for a long moment then shook his head. "Meigh? No, our proposals were radical, we discussed them in depth . . ."

"Nothing."

"But she wouldn't have . . ."

Dehan snapped, "Wouldn't have what? Are you saying she kept stuff back?"

"I don't know, man. I'm just a student. I'm not even a graduate. You'd have to ask her . . ."

I pressed him. "But you are certain that he had proposals that were revolutionary."

"I don't know."

"You just said so."

"Yeah, but you just said . . ."

"Were you lying?"

"No, man! Stop it!"

"Think very carefully before you answer, Am. Did you and Robles discuss research that he was conducting that would be a radical improvement to the lithium-ion battery?"

He swallowed. "Yes. We did."

"And you were involved in that research?"

"Yes."

"Where did he go Saturday nights?"

He stared at me and went a sallow gray color. "What?"

"Where did Robles go Saturday nights?"

"I don't know. I have no idea. How would I know?"

"I need you to come to the station and make a statement."

"Now? I have a late seminar. I have a ton of work to do, man. I'll be there first thing in the morning. Nine o'clock."

"We'll take you and bring you back."

"C'mon, man! Give me a break! I told you I'm struggling with my reputation here. If I'm seen leaving with the cops..."

I sighed. "Nine a.m., I want to see you there. And don't even dream about changing your story."

"I'll be there. I promise."

We walked back out into the dark. Little spits of freezing rain were being carried on the air by a light breeze. We climbed into the car. I fired her up and we pulled away toward the Bronx. The traffic was at its heaviest and we crawled along, stopping and starting among the broken, wet lights. I took out my cell and called the inspector.

"John, where are you? I've had Costas on the phone twice in the last hour."

"We're stuck in traffic, sir. We should be there within the hour."

"I'll tell him to make his way over, then."

"Yes, sir, we'll be as quick as we can."

At Madison Square Park, however, I took a left and cruised slowly down West 25th. Dehan didn't say anything because she knew what I was doing. I turned right on 8th and then right again onto West 26th. I slowed as we approached number 250. It was the Wells Fargo building. Above it there was a jiujitsu club, and above that was Dare 2 Dream, the club Dr. Jose Robles used to frequent on Saturday nights.

It was ten to eight by the time we got back to the station. We found the assistant district attorney in the inspector's office. He stood to greet us as we stripped off our coats.

"John, Carmen, thank you for meeting with me. I know it's a long day."

His manner and his voice were pleasant. He was in his forties, balding slightly, but his hair was still black. We sat, and he studied first Dehan and then me. "How did you get on?"

Dehan made a ball of her hat and said, "Before we get onto that, may I ask you a question, sir?"

"Of course, but please, call me Costas."

"Have you a personal interest in this case?"

His face hardened. "What are you suggesting, Detective?"

"I'm not suggesting anything, sir. I'm just asking if you have a personal interest in the case." He sighed and sat back in his chair. Dehan went on. "We would like to know what prompted you to press for a continuation of this investigation, rather than accepting Detective Gutierrez's conclusions. That's a very unusual thing to do."

He said, carefully, "There seemed to be unexplained aspects to the case."

"Could you give us an example, sir?"

He hesitated. "You pointed out yourselves, the gun. Not only was it an unusual choice for a woman like Agnes, but where did she get it from? Also, where is she? It is not easy to disappear that completely in this day and age, even for a professional criminal. Yet she has vanished without leaving a trace. Her cards have not been used. There has been a BOLO out on her and on her car for a couple of weeks, but there is not a trace of her."

Dehan leaned forward with her elbows on her knees and nodded several times. "Sir, Costas, my partner and I run the cold-cases unit in this precinct. Our archive isn't computerized yet, so it still fills two big cartons with cases. Some of them go back thirty years. What is it about this one, in particular, that makes it more important than all those other cases?"

He stared for a long time at the floor. The inspector was looking hard at Dehan. Finally, Costas said, "You are quite right, Detective, and you have a right to know. Jose was a friend of mine. When I heard he had been murdered, it was a huge shock, and the more I looked at the murder scene, the less convincing I found it. Gutierrez is a good detective, but I asked John to put somebody on it who would look beneath the obvious." He gestured at us with both hands. "I see he made a good choice."

She gave a humorless snort. "One thing you can say for this case is that there is nothing obvious about it. It seems everybody has half a story to tell." He frowned at her, and she held his eye, then said, "Dr. Meigh made Dr. Robles' research available to us. We examined it. Obviously a lot of it was incomprehensible to us, but that part of it which was translated into layman's terms seemed unremarkable. She left us alone with it without supervision, and if we had wanted to, we could have photographed and copied it. Her security was not lax, it was nonexistent." She paused. "Another thing that struck us both as surprising was that the research was stored at her house."

"That is surprising."

The inspector gave me a curious look. "I don't know what common practice is in these cases, but you'd expect . . ."

"Unless the value of the work he was doing was not as great as they are making out. On the other hand, she is the head of the department and in charge of the project." I shook my head. "I honestly don't know. What I do know is that what we saw was little more than a review of existing technology."

Costas looked from me to Dehan and back again. "Not a motive for murder, then?"

I shook my head. "Not what we saw, no."

He hesitated. "What are your conclusions, so far?"

"We haven't any, so far. We have three major questions: Where is Agnes Shine? How did she get hold of that gun? And who is Mohamed?"

His face went rigid. "Mohamed?"

"Yes, Mohamed."

He shook his head. "I don't understand. I mean, I can only repeat your question. Who is Mohamed? How have you come up with this name?"

I watched him carefully as Dehan said, "He is somebody who was in touch with Dr. Robles and seems to have been threatening him."

"With what?"

I said, "With exposure?"

"Exposure? What kind of exposure?"

"That's what we don't know. Can you offer us any insight into that?"

"No. I mean, how would I?"

"You were friends."

"But not that . . . I mean, not close enough to know anything that might be *exposed*!"

I spread my hands. "That's where the investigation is at the moment, Costas."

He stared at the floor a moment. "Yes, I see. Well . . ." He stood and took his coat from the back of his chair. "I'll let you get home. Thank you for meeting with me."

I stood. "If, as his friend, you should think of anything that could help us, however unrelated . . ."

He nodded. "I know the routine, Detective. Thanks again." He turned to the inspector. "John, thanks again for your help."

He left and closed the door behind him. We heard his feet on the stairs, and after a moment, the inspector raised his eyebrows at us. "Would you mind telling me what that was about?"

Dehan still had her elbows on her knees, turning her hat over in her hands. She glanced at me. I said, "I wish I knew, sir."

He shook his head. "Uh-uh, that won't do, John. When you subject the assistant district attorney to that kind of treatment in my office, and he takes it, I am entitled to know why!"

I sat. My ankles were cold, and I could see amber droplets of rain spattering the window overlooking Story Avenue. Suddenly I wanted to be at home in front of the fire, smelling something good coming from the kitchen. I sighed.

"Truthfully, sir, all I can tell you is that there seemed to be a portion of Dr. Robles' research missing, that Dr. Meigh and Dr. Shine were close friends, but Dr. Meigh lied about it, that Dr. Robles frequented a nightclub on West Twenty-Sixth Street, in Chelsea, most Saturday nights, that somebody called Mohamed threatened to join one of his classes, and that ADA Costas Varoufakis is hiding something, but I have no idea what. That, right now, is the extent of my knowledge."

He stared at me a moment then waved his hands in the air and shook his head. "Fine! Fine! We could probably all do with going home and having a good night's sleep."

I looked over at Dehan. She looked as dead beat as I felt. "Unfortunately, sir," I said, "we still have to go dancing tonight."

TEN

We arrived on West 26th at midnight. Dare 2 Dream was located discreetly on the top floor and sported a vast terrace, a lawn, palm trees, and even a swimming pool, all under a glass dome annexed to the bar. There was no music as such. It was more as though some electronic god had gone into paroxysmal supraventricular tachycardia and we were trapped inside his chest. There were a lot of people, and most of them were bouncing. The ones that weren't bouncing were leaning into each other's ears and shouting, then nodding at each other with faces that seemed to say, *I have no idea what you just said*.

As we squeezed through the press of bouncing, squinting people, I began to notice a third group. These were dressed mainly in black leather. It was not overt, but if you were looking for the signs, they were there. Mainly they were in dark corners, behind palms or partly concealed by groups of voyeurs.

Dehan grabbed my head and leaned in close to my ear. "Is it a gay club? I can't work it out!"

I shook my head and put my mouth to her ear. "No! It's a dare to dream club. Whatever you're into! What Mo would call bacon, lettuce, and tomato!"

She shouted back: "You think they cater to straight, monogamous chicks?"

"I hope so. Come on, I need a drink."

We pushed toward the bar, which was made of translucent blue glass, and found a spot where I could hail the barperson. The barperson had a small knitting needle through her nose and dead people tattooed on her arms. She wiped the space in front of us and said, "Get you?"

"Two Bushmills, straight up."

She poured them swiftly and efficiently and said, "Forty bucks!"

I handed her fifty and said, "Is Mohamed in tonight?"

In my peripheral vision, I saw Dehan stare at me. Barperson took my money and frowned. "Pal, there must be five hundred people here right now. How the hell would I know?"

I shrugged, and on an impulse I said, "Ali said you knew him."

"Ali? Mohamed? What is this, ISIS revenge? Gimme a break, willya?"

She took the money to the till and rung it up. Dehan leaned over to me and said, "Have you gone crazy?"

"I'm testing a theory."

The barperson came back with my change. She handed it to me and said, "Ali? What's this Ali like?"

"Spanish, pretty, short hair . . ."

"Talks too much?"

I laughed. "Yeah."

"She said I knew Mohamed? What else she say?"

I shrugged. "She told me to talk to you." I turned to Dehan. "What else did she say, honey?"

Dehan winked at the barperson. "She said you would help us, and that you were a *tía buena*."

She shrugged her tattooed shoulder and shook her head. "I don't know what that means."

"It means you're hot."

Now she gave a bashful, lopsided smile and pointed toward a

palm by the door to the dome. There was a table in the shadows beside it with several people sitting there. "He usually sits over there. You know what he looks like? Big, six-three, tattoos like mine. Got short hair and very blue eyes."

I shook my head. "Not an Arab?"

Barperson's laugh was scornful. "No, dude." To Dehan she said, "Name's Heimdall. I get off at three."

Dehan grinned. "Carmen. I'll be around."

"Carmen, that's nice."

We elbowed and shouldered our way through the crowd toward the palm. Dehan was tugging on my sleeve. I looked back at her and mouthed, *Wait!*

When we got to the table by the palm, the music wasn't as loud. There were four guys sitting there. Two were on stools, the other two on a padded bench against the wall. One of them was huge. He had the tattoos, very short hair, and even from where I was standing, I could see his eyes were a very pale blue. He had on a gray, string-sleeved vest, and one of his massive arms was around another guy who must have been half his size and half his weight and was wearing false eyelashes and very red lipstick. They all looked up as we arrived. They seemed more interested in Dehan than in me, but the interest was not all that friendly.

I jerked my head toward the big guy. "You Mohamed?"

He lounged back with his mouth slightly open. "No, I'm Thomas fuckin' Aquinas. Who the fuck are you, apart from the guy who's gonna . . ."

I held up a hand. "Before we get there, Robles sent me with a message."

"You're a lying fuckin' bastard."

"Yeah? Maybe I am at that. How about we go out to the lawn and talk about it out there?"

"Yeah?" He looked at his pals and they all laughed. "How about I break your arms and legs and throw you off the fuckin' roof?"

"How about you try? Either way, let's do it outside."

He got to his feet, and before he could reach for me, I moved to the door and opened it. Dehan stepped out onto the terrace, and as he came around the palm, flexing his muscles, I pulled my jacket back just enough for him to see the butt of my Colt. I smiled sweetly at him and jerked my head at the door. "Outside, Mohamed."

"What the fuck . . . ?"

"Outside."

He went out after Dehan, and his friends made to follow. I pointed a finger like a gun at them and said, "Scram!" Then I followed Mohamed out and let the door close behind me. The noise was less: a mild throb in the background, behind the hiss and hum of the traffic in the street below.

Dehan had moved to a table by a heater and was sitting, sipping her drink, watching me curiously. Mohamed was still standing, facing me as I approached him. "Who are you, man? What's the deal with Robles? I ain't spoken to him since . . ."

"Since what? Sit down, Mohamed."

He narrowed his eyes a moment then moved to the table and sat. He stared at Dehan, calculating, then looked at me. "Since he deleted me from Telegram. Who are you . . . ?"

I grinned. "You're asking, but you've guessed already, haven't you?"

"You're cops. I don't know what that son of a bitch has said to you, but he told me to leave him alone and I have left him alone."

"You threatened to join his class. You knew how that could affect his career."

"Hey, man!" He spread his hands and hunched his shoulders. "Words! It was a lovers' spat. I was hurting. Lovers say that kind of thing. But when I realized he was serious and it was over, I left it."

"What did you want from him?"

"I wanted him to come out. I just wanted him to admit to the world that he loved me. Is that a lot to ask? Instead it was always this big macho act. Until he got behind the bedroom door. Then the whole story changed. He'd get on his knees and beg like a dog if I told him to."

"I don't need the details."

"Your loss."

"No doubt. Who else was in his crowd of friends?"

"Oh, you want me to be a snitch?" He looked at Dehan. She smiled at him. He looked back at me. "What is this, Trump's little private army? Out to exterminate the deviants? Start with the college professors and purify the race?"

I shook my head and showed him my badge. "I'm Detective Stone. This is my partner, Detective Dehan. We have no interest in your sex life, Mohamed, but I'm afraid I have to tell you that Dr. Jose Robles was murdered last week, and we are trying to find his killer."

His jaw sagged in a tragic echo of his expression when he'd first spoken to me. Arrogance was now replaced by shock, and that slowly began to give way to uncomprehending grief. His lower lip curled; his eyes became puffy and wet. His voice became a twisted whine.

"Why . . . ?" He looked from Dehan to me again, wanting an answer, suddenly like a child denied its most treasured toy. "No . . . Why . . . ? Not Jose . . . !"

He sat with his hands limp on his lap and his head thrown up to the glass dome, making a strange guttural noise designed to persuade a disinterested, uninterested, heartless god not to steal away his dreams. I sighed and glanced at Dehan. Her expression was hard to read. I said to Mohamed:

"Come on, we'll take you to the station and give you some coffee. I need you to make a statement."

He shook his head. "No. I want to be here, with my people. My friends. I'm not going anywhere. If you want to ask me questions, you'll have to ask them here."

"All right, who was in Dr. Robles' crowd of friends, who used to come here?"

He ran the back of his hand across his eyes. "He used to come a lot with Ali. She was wild. I loved her. We used to joke that we were the Taliban. Ali and Mohamed. The terrorists. That was her joke mainly. She was like his beard. Then, more recently, just before we . . ." The tears spilled from his eyes and he shook his head at me, his eyes narrowed with resentment, his voice barely audible. "We could have been good, we could have been happy . . ."

I said, "A short guy, trim, in his forties, balding black hair, Mediterranean look?"

He nodded. "He was flaunting him at me. He was so cruel sometimes!"

"This guy have a name?"

"Most people don't use names here."

"But you knew Dr. Robles' name. You knew everything about him."

He shrugged. His face, his voice, were helpless, bewildered. "We were a couple. We were going to get an apartment. We were solid. I told him everything, and he shared everything with me. Then one day, it was just after we'd had a beautiful weekend together, he turned up with this . . . My god! He looked like a *lawyer*!"

"Think before you answer, Mohamed. Was this guy gay?"

"Well, if he wasn't, he was sure putting on a good show! They were dancing and kissing like they meant it."

I pulled out my cell, found a picture of Assistant DA Costas Varoufakis, and expanded it so there was no information visible. I showed it to Mohamed. "This the guy?"

He nodded. "Yeah, that's him. Who is he?"

I put the phone away. "What's your name?"

"Am I under arrest?"

"No, but you might be a witness to a murder. What's your name?"

"Daniel Brand."

"I need your phone number and your address, and I need you at the Forty-Third Precinct tomorrow no later than ten to make a statement. You understand that? You don't show, there will be a BOLO out for you."

Anger suddenly constricted his face. "Hey! Pal! I ain't a criminal! You don't need to threaten me. I'll do my civic duty, okay?"

I nodded. "Okay." I went to stand, then stopped. "Just a couple more questions. Did he ever come here with another woman?"

He shook his head. "The only woman he came with was Ali."

"Did he ever show any interest in buying a gun?"

I might have asked if he ate babies for breakfast. The look of horror transfigured his face. "Are you *crazy*? Jose was just totally, totally anti guns! He even hated bullfighting! And believe me, he was so Spanish! But he detested all forms of violence . . . unless they were consensual."

I looked at Dehan. She raised her eyebrows and shook her head. I said, "Okay, let's go."

We stood and made our way back to the bar. As we went through the door, Mohamed's friends pushed past us and ran out to him. Heimdall didn't see us leave.

Dehan didn't speak in the elevator or in the lobby. She waited till we were out in the street and I was unlocking the car. Then she leaned on the roof, with the icy wind whipping her hair across her face, and said, "How? *How* did you know? How could you *possibly* have known?"

I opened the door and climbed in the car. She got in the other side and slammed the door after her. For a moment we were cocooned in a comfortable silence. I started the engine and pulled away.

"The simple answer is that I didn't."

"No, uh-uh." She shook her head and wagged her finger in the negative. "No. No, sir. You knew, and I'll tell you something else, you came here for the express purpose of meeting Mohamed, because you knew that he would be here. Deny it."

I smiled. "I deny it. I had a hunch, but it wasn't that hard to see, Dehan. You would have seen it too if you had stopped talking yourself in circles."

"Talking myself in circles . . ."

She didn't say it resentfully. She frowned like she was thinking about it.

I nodded. "Yes, you had two theories you were considering, the terrorist or jealous Agnes. But we realized almost from the start that Mohamed could not be a terrorist, or an industrial spy in the employ of the Saudis. Two things stood out: on the one hand, there was the fact that he had deleted the Telegram app, which we agreed he would not have been allowed to do if he was negotiating with Middle Eastern interests. And on the other hand, the nature of the message itself. It was a threat, for sure, but not a threat to kill or torture him. It was a threat by Mohamed to reveal his existence at Robles' workplace. It was Mohamed's *existence* that was the threat. Add that to Robles' rather odd relationship with Agnes and it's not a huge leap to a gay lover."

She sighed. "So obvious . . ."

I shrugged. "Well, that and my razor-like mind."

"Yeah, that too. So where the hell does that leave us? I am still no clearer, Stone."

The roads were almost empty and we made good time. We crossed at the Madison Avenue Bridge and headed north on 3rd Avenue and Boston Road. I didn't answer her because I didn't know how to. I had found a corner and a patch of sky in the puzzle, but it still didn't make any kind of picture. There were two disparate parts to it: the sex and the science. And there didn't seem to be any way to make them match up and make sense.

"It leaves us with a man," I said, and Dehan looked startled because we had been quiet for almost fifteen minutes, "who stirred up intense feelings in people, feelings of love, devotion, anger, hatred and contempt. It leaves us with a man who did all of that through his public persona, while keeping his private self well hidden. His private self was, by all accounts, a brilliant scientist, about whom we know practically nothing. It leaves us wondering which one of the two got him killed."

ELEVEN

The next morning, at ten to nine, we were in interview room three drinking coffee. I was sitting at the table, and Dehan was leaning with her back against the wall, her arms folded. We were waiting for Am Nielsen to arrive, and Dehan was speaking our thoughts for us.

"We have a serious question we need to decide, Stone, and we need to make up our minds by the time we finish taking Am's statement. We need to decide whether we tell the chief about Costas and Jose."

I nodded and looked at my shoes. They had no answers for me. "For that, we need to decide if his affair with Robles is relevant to the case. So far it's only relevant to his getting us on the case."

"Is it?"

"Honestly, I don't know."

"There is another question, which frankly he dodged last night, about *why* he was so convinced the case needed to be looked into more deeply. I mean, let's face it, the fact that he and Robles were lovers makes it more likely, not less, that Agnes killed him. One thing is being dumped for another woman—at least Ali is gorgeous and shared all of Robles' tastes and prejudices—but to be dumped for a guy? That's got to hurt. That could tip a neurotic woman over the edge."

"It's a good point."

"And it's an important question." She stated it with emphasis: "What made Costas so convinced that Agnes did not kill Dr. Robles?"

I nodded. "It is an important question, the more so because he must have known, when he pressed the chief, that a deeper investigation risked revealing his relationship with Robles."

She shrugged. "I don't see any option. We have to tell him."

"Let's get Am and Mohamed out of the way, then we'll talk to the inspector about Costas and where the case seems to be going." I sighed and held up both hands, like I was holding two oranges. "There's his personality and his sex life, here, on the left. And then there is his research, here, on the right. On the left you have Mohamed, Ali, Agnes, and Costas Varoufakis. On the right you have his actual, physical research, the bit that's missing, Dr. Meigh, and Am." I paused. "Thinking aloud, we originally thought that Mohamed was on the right, but he turned out to be part of his sex life."

We were quiet for a while, staring at the empty place in space where we both imagined the small clusters of people and facts. Then Dehan said, "Maybe that's just it, Stone. Maybe they are, in actual fact, separate. Maybe there is no connection between the two. Maybe he had such a damned awful attitude, such a conflictive approach to life, that he generated hostility and problems wherever he went. And that is what gives us the illusion that it is all connected to his death."

I frowned. "Explain."

"Okay, the world is divided into those who thought Robles was great, and those who thought he was a royal pain in the ass. Now, just imagine, a department of nice, nerdy scientists who all get on together and either have chess evenings smoking pipes or play *Lord of the Rings* and *Halo* games together. They are all happy in Nerd Land. And then, one day, El Grincho comes along, sneering at everything, putting everybody down, playing his power games, insulting everybody, and generally being a pain in the butt. Everybody wants him to leave, but there's a problem."

I said, "He's a very good scientist and he is contributing radical ideas to the research."

"Exactly. So they have to put up with him. That's what's going on in the right-hand bubble. Now, meantime, in the left-hand bubble, we see that his desire to put everybody down and play power games is nothing more than an expression of his sexual proclivities."

"Who are you? And what have you done with Dehan? Where did you learn such language?"

"I told you, from your books. Robles has a compulsive, sexual need to dominate people or be dominated by them. This draws people like Agnes into a dependent relationship with him. She needs him, badly, but he refuses to get involved with her romantically, yet at the same time refuses to set her free. Double bind. The first humiliation comes in the form of Ali, and then the final straw is Mohamed and/or Costas. She snaps and kills him." I drew breath but she held up a hand. "*Meanwhile*, presented with his death, Dr. Meigh does two things. One, she shelters Agnes, and two, she holds back the key part of his research, planning to present it later as either her own or the work of the team. The team quietly acquiesce—all, that is, but Am Nielsen."

I thought about it for a while. Finally, I said, "That is a very compelling piece of reasoning, Dehan. I like it very much. It's brilliant."

"Gee. Shucks, boss."

I glanced at her. "What about the gun?"

"As you would say, two gets you twenty she got that from Dr. Meigh. We need to look into her. Maybe her husband was a marine, or at least military. My bet is she got it from her old pal Meigh, who later sheltered her."

I thought about the man I'd seen Meigh kiss and hand over the keys to the Audi. He didn't look especially lethal, but you couldn't always tell. "If that's true, then it elevates Meigh's involvement to conspiracy to commit murder."

"Yeah."

I looked at my watch. It was five past nine. "He's late." We stared at each other for a moment. "Once we have his testimony, we go back to Meigh and demand to see the missing part of the research."

"What about Mohamed?"

"We'll get Gomez to take it. I want to talk to Meigh before they go on holiday."

Dehan gave a single nod. "If we can get her to admit to that much, maybe we can use it as leverage to force her to give up Agnes . . ." We stared at each other a moment longer and she shrugged. "That's what this whole thing comes down to now, Stone, isn't it? Find Agnes."

"I guess . . ." I looked at my watch again. Ten past. I pulled out my cell and called Am. I got a message saying it was switched off or out of range. "He's not coming."

She frowned. "Come on! He's probably on the subway."

I shook my head. "He's not coming. Get your woolly hat, Dehan. I'm going to call Hays and try Am again. You put out a BOLO and arrange for a car to go to the university. We're going to his house."

She stood, looking at me as though I'd gone crazy. "*Why?* He's ten minutes late, Stone!"

"Because we are missing something and I don't know what it is. But believe me, he is not coming!"

I ran down the stairs dialing Hays' number. It rang a couple of times before he answered.

"You again, Detective."

"Yeah, me again. Is Am Nielsen there? Have you seen him today?"

"He isn't here, and I haven't seen him. He's probably still in bed. It's barely a quarter past nine!"

"I know what time it is. The moment you see him, you call me. Tell him to stay put. I'll come and get him."

"Is that an order?"

"Yes."

His tone was sarcastic; mine wasn't. I hung up and went to the detectives' room to grab my coat. When I stepped outside, it had started to drizzle, but the drizzle was turning to a fine sleet. I opened the door, and Dehan came out of the station, swaddled in wool, and ran across the road to join me. As we climbed in, she said, "Time to share, big guy. You know it makes me mad when you cut me out."

I reversed out of the lot, turned into Metcalf, crossed the Bruckner Expressway, and joined the boulevard on the other side, going west. There I hit the gas, headed for Hunts Point.

"I don't know, Dehan. I'm as confused as you are. Everything you said makes sense. But Am doesn't make sense. He doesn't fit with the logical explanation. I can't put it into words for you right now, but I know he's gone as sure as I know I had coffee this morning." I glanced at her. "It's at least twenty past now, right?"

She checked her watch. "Yeah, twenty-two."

"Call the station, call the university, call him. I'll tell you what you'll find. He hasn't showed, and his cell is either out of range or switched off."

She waited a second, then pulled out her phone and called the station. She put it on speaker.

"Maria, this is Detective Dehan. Has Am Nielsen turned up yet?"

"No, no word from him yet."

"Call me when he shows, will you?"

"You told me that five minutes ago, honey."

She called Hays.

"Dr. Hays, this is Detective Dehan . . ."

"Your partner spoke to me five minutes ago and ordered me to telephone him as soon as Nielsen arrived. He has not arrived. As soon as he does, I will call you. Is there anything else the police state would like from me before I start my day's work?"

"No, thank you."

She called Am and got no response.

Under the overpass, I turned onto Hunts Point Avenue and accelerated toward his house. I pulled up outside just as Dehan's cell started to ring. She climbed out and slammed the door as she answered it.

"Yeah, Dehan." She listened, watching me as I went to the door, hammered, and rang the bell. "Okay," she said. "Just stand by. Wait there for now."

The drapes were closed and there was no sound from inside. Suddenly Dehan shrugged. "It's simple, Stone."

"What is?"

"He supplied the gun. It was staring us in the face. I think one of us actually said it right at the beginning, but we dismissed it."

"Why would he?"

She put her hands on my chest. Puffs of condensation came from her mouth as she spoke. "Put it together. He told us he liked her. He's a chameleon. We've seen he has the ability to adapt to whatever he thinks people expect from him. Hell, he played us! He had us eating soup with him, listening to his story, and advising him to go back to college! He even got that arrogant bastard Robles to get him onto the research team. So he got himself inside Agnes' head."

"What for?"

"I can give you two reasons. One, to help him get close to Robles because Robles could advance his career. It was not Robles who took an interest in Nielsen, but Nielsen who took an interest in Robles. And two, because Agnes is in fact an attractive woman."

I frowned. "Agnes Shine?"

"Have you seen a picture of her?"

"She's pretty enough, but she's nothing special, Dehan."

Her expression became smug. "Except, look at the way people

respond to her. Ali looks like a million bucks, but how do people respond to her? With indifference. Agnes on the other hand, quiet, shy, retiring Agnes gets invited to the Meighs' every weekend, becomes Robles' special friend, Hays' special friend, has Patricia Meigh hiding her, *and* has Nielsen paying her special attention. I'm telling you, partner, Agnes Shine has a special attraction *because* of her shy, vulnerable nature. And Am Nielsen liked her, and with his empathic nature, he got inside her defenses, and when she decided she'd had enough of Robles she went to him—not Dr. Meigh or her husband!—to Am Nielsen because she knew *he* could get her a gun. And *that*, my friend, resolves the mystery of the Sig Sauer Tacops P226, unregistered and hot off the station wagon from Colorado."

I thought about it for a moment. "You're on fire today, Dehan. So wherever he is now . . ."

"She might be there too!" She pulled her cell and walked toward the car dialing. I called the inspector.

"John, good morning!"

I put him up to speed as far as Am was concerned and said, "I need to get into his house. There is a chance that Agnes is in there, or that there is some indication of where she might be."

"Yes, I agree. I'll send a crime scene team over too. Let's see if there is any trace of her there."

"Good, thank you, sir."

I hung up and, by applying the small screwdriver on my Swiss Army knife, opened the lock before Dehan got back.

"We got probable cause?"

"The chief thinks so. We have a crime scene team coming over to look for traces of Agnes. You got gloves?"

"Always, baby."

I glanced at her. Her tone of voice was incongruent with her wool elf look. She grinned. "I got the techs searching for his GPS. As soon as they find him, they'll let us know."

The kitchen showed us nothing but a pot of soup, one bowl, and one spoon washed and dried on the rack. There was also a coffee percolator on the stove. I opened it and checked the grains. They were dry. The cups were all dry too, and stored away.

"He didn't make coffee this morning."

"That's bad."

"The last meal he had was soup."

She smelled it. "It's not rancid, but in this cold, that doesn't mean much. It could be last night's or the night before." She put the pot down and faced me. "We spoke to him yesterday evening. We spooked him. He didn't want to make a statement. He was anxious to get away. He bolted as soon as we left."

I nodded. "Let's have a look in the bedroom. See if he's packed."

The bed was unmade. His phone charger was plugged in next to the clock. I touched Dehan's arm and pointed to it. She opened the wardrobe. There were a couple of jackets, a suit, a tie, some shirts, some chinos, shoes, and boots. Two sports bags lay on the bottom of the wardrobe.

I opened the drawers in the tallboy against the wall. His underwear, his socks, jeans, belts, and sweaters were all there. In the bathroom, his toothbrush, hairbrush, and razor were all there. Dehan said:

"He didn't come home to pack. He was in a hurry."

"I don't see his computer. He must have had it with him. But he's left everything else." I sighed and leaned my back against the wall. "What did we talk about? What did we say that could have spooked him so much?"

She thought for a minute. Outside the window, I could hear the cold sound of water spattering on the sidewalk from the guttering above. Dehan stuffed her hat in her pocket.

"He talked about how he was a clown, how they'd all heard Dr. Shine was a suspect in Robles' murder. He knew Robles treated her like crap. He didn't like that. He said she was really sweet—he used those words—and there was no way she shot him. He said he was sure Robles' death had something to do with the research they were doing, but he had no concrete evidence, it was just a hunch. So he knew if he called us and said he was Robles' student and believed Agnes was innocent, with no hard facts, we wouldn't listen to him . . ."

"But that's what he said; what did we say? Something we said spooked him."

"I'm trying to remember. He said he got caught up playing a part . . . We asked him how much of what he said was true; he said pretty much all of it, he was from Colorado, his name, his dad . . ."

"You asked him if Robles had intervened on his behalf. That was when he told us it was not to get into the university, but onto the research program, remember? We asked if he had a good relationship with Robles . . ."

She pointed at me. "He said it was very good and confirmed they had plans for the Robles-Americano . . ."

". . . And that was when I told him that there was research missing from what Meigh had shown us. That was when he started to get anxious, when I asked him to confirm, in a statement, that Robles' research was radical and revolutionary."

She nodded. "That, and when you asked him where Robles went on Saturday nights."

I shook my head. "I can't see it, Dehan. I can't see anything there that would spook him enough to make him run."

She nodded. "I can."

"Tell me."

"If Agnes has got Dr. Meigh and Am Nielsen to help her—Dr. Meigh to hide her and Am to provide her with a weapon—it is possible, even probable, that Meigh doesn't know anything about Am or how he got her the gun, but it is almost certain that Am knew that Meigh was hiding her."

"Possible."

"So when he hears that Meigh has started messing with the research, and we know about it, he figures we are going to start investigating her, and it's now only a matter of time before we find that she is hiding Agnes. You still with me? He's a chess player, remember? He's thinking several moves ahead. He knows that in a few moves we will have Agnes, she will confess and tell us where she got the gun from. So he bolts."

I stared at her. "So Am gives Agnes the gun, Meigh doesn't know that. When Robles dies, she hides his crucial research so she can present it as her own, we get wise to that, and he fears our investigation into Meigh will show he was an accomplice in Robles' murder..."

Before she could answer, her phone rang. She pulled it from her pocket and put it on speaker. "Yeah, Dehan."

"Detective, we have just picked up a very weak signal from Mr. Nielsen's phone."

"Where?"

"I think he must be on a barge, Detective, because the signal keeps fading and coming back, like it's being shielded by lead or something. He's on the river."

"Which river?"

"North stretch of the Harlem, where it branches off the Hudson? Right by the Columbia University athletic complex. I'm sending you the coordinates to your phone. There's a jetty there in the park, and he seems to be moored there."

Her phone pinged and she said, "Okay, got it."

Outside, I could hear the crime scene team arriving. I sighed and reached for my phone. "We'd better call for backup. I think we could have trouble."

TWELVE

By the time we got to West 218th, the signal from Am's GPS had grown a little stronger. Access to the Inwood Hill Park, where the pier was located, was cut off by two bollards and six artistically placed rocks. We stopped there, and two patrol cars pulled in behind us. Dehan climbed out and pointed up the road, shouting to the nearest car.

"Campbell, you and O'Connor take the other corner! GPS says he's still on the boat, cover the paths in case he tries to run!" The car took off up the road. "Mendez! Wagner, with me!"

With that, Dehan and I took off at a run through the park, with Mendez and Wagner close behind. It was three hundred yards, and the air was cold and rasped in my throat and lungs.

The pier was located in a small bay that cut into a spit of land that protruded into the northernmost stretch of the Harlem River. At low tide, the bay was simply a stretch of mud some two hundred yards across, with a small wooden pier, half-concealed by trees, poking out from the parkland near the baseball pitch. When we got there and rounded the tree cover, Dehan stopped dead, and Mendez and Wagner stopped behind her. We were all panting big billows of frosted air. There was no water in the bay, only mud. And there was no boat, no barge sitting on the sludge, waiting for the high tide.

Dehan shook her head. "There's nothing there."

I nodded. "There is, we just can't see it yet."

She frowned at me, and I walked across the scrubby grass and onto the pier. Dehan, Mendez, and Wagner followed close behind. I reached the end and looked down. It wasn't visible at first. Dehan stared uncomprehending at the expanse of gray mire and shallow streams of water that trickled through it.

I turned to Wagner and said, "Call it in, Linda. We need a meat wagon, the ME, and a crime scene team. Tell them where the body is; they'll need planks or something to get out there. And tell them they're on the clock. The tide will be coming in again." She was frowning at me. I pointed to a narrow, shallow stream near the foot of the pier, which was draining slowly out into the river. "He's there, in the water. Call it in."

She called Dispatch. Dehan was leaning on the rail, squinting at the stream. "I wouldn't have seen him if you hadn't pointed him out. I would have assumed he'd dumped his phone." She looked up at me. "You knew what to look for. You were expecting it."

"I knew there were no barges up here. What your tech said made no sense. The Harlem is a tidal strait. The fact that the signal was emerging slowly suggested the phone had been submerged, and the tide was going out. Water will block the signal unless it is very shallow."

"Elementary . . ."

"But there's one thing that isn't so elementary. Even the most water-resistant of phones won't last much more than half an hour underwater. If his is still working, it means it's in some kind of watertight container. Which is kind of odd."

"Why the hell . . . !"

I shook my head and grinned. "Not why, Little Grasshopper, what. What would make him, or his killer, wrap his phone in plastic before either he was thrown, or he jumped, into the river?"

She sighed and rolled her eyes. "Yes! Okay! You're right! It works. The only reason would be to ensure that it was found in working order."

"And the only purpose for that would be if it contains information the suicide, or the killer, wants us to have."

"Just when I thought I had it figured."

I leaned my elbows next to hers and shuddered as the cold crept up my arms. "You never know," I said. "It might confirm your theory."

There was a touch of resentment in her face. "My theory? It's not our theory?"

I took a deep breath and looked down at the hand that was slowly becoming more visible as the water drained out of the channel. "I don't know, Dehan. I just don't know. There is still something missing. We need to establish whether he was murdered or committed suicide. If he committed suicide, that will tend to confirm your theory. It also suggests a reason for keeping the phone dry, doesn't it?"

"Yes, it does . . . What?"

I laughed. "A millennial suicide note."

"Wow, and you're the dinosaur."

"Don't knock the dinosaurs, kid. We survived almost two hundred million years. How long have you puny humans been around?"

She observed me with hooded eyes and pointed to the path that ran through the park. "Here comes the puny medical examiner, and the puny crime scene team is close behind him."

They worked fast and laid a path of wooden planking out to where the body was half-covered in silt and muddy water. The scene itself had little to tell them. What little evidence there may have been had been washed away by the tide. The body was recovered, bagged, and brought ashore, then laid on a gurney. As we approached, Frank unzipped the bag to expose the face. It was bloated and a gray-blue color, but it was easily recognizable.

"That's Am Nielsen."

Frank looked at me curiously. "Am?" I nodded. He zipped up the bag and said, "Am is now Was. Which proves just how relative time is."

Dehan asked him, "Can you tell us anything?"

"Not really, Carmen. On the face of it, there don't appear to be any bullet wounds or stab wounds. Bruising is hard to establish until I have washed him off. He looks as though he has drowned, but until I get him on the table, I can't say for sure."

"Has your wife divorced you yet, Frank?"

He arched an eyebrow at her. "All of them. Why?"

"So you have time to work on him tonight, right?"

"What do you see in her, Stone? She has no soul."

"That's an advantage in a woman, Frank. The soul of Woman was created below. You should know that. Can you? He was a witness in the Robles case. ADA Costas Varoufakis has a personal interest."

The body was loaded in and the ambulance pulled away. Frank pulled off his gloves. "Varoufakis? Seriously? If you were called Varoufakis, wouldn't you change your name? I would."

He climbed in his car and slammed the door. Then the window slid down and he leaned out. "Drop by this evening on your way home. I might have made a start by then."

We watched him drive away through the park. When he was gone from view, Dehan said, "I've been avoiding making any comment about the ADA's name since we first took the case."

I heard a shout behind me and saw Joe approaching from where his guys were working on the pier.

"Stone, I was going to phone you, then the call came in and I thought I'd see you here."

"What you got, Joe?"

"First of all, the phone. You were right. He had it sealed in a watertight bag in his jacket. Go figure. We've kept the bag for printing. Here it is . . ." He fished it out of the pocket of his white spaceman suit, contained in an evidence bag. ". . . in another plastic bag. I figured you'd want to look at the contents.

If you want the guys at the lab to have a look, send it back to me."

"I appreciate it."

"Now, I was going to call you; you asked me to find whose saliva was on the glasses, back at the original crime scene."

"Yeah, that's right."

He gave a small laugh and shook his head. "Odd, but nobody's was. Not on her glass, and not on his."

Dehan pointed a woolen finger at me. "Ha! That is not as surprising as you might think!"

Joe laughed. "Really? Why's that?"

"He was a wine snob. Only Spanish wine from Ribera del Duero or La Rioja was good enough for him. This wine was, let me see if I can remember . . ." I drew breath and she snapped, "Don't! It was Bogle Vineyards, 2016, and he probably refused to drink it. Simple." She thought about it for a second. "And you know what? That small, final act of arrogance might just have been the small straw that finally broke the camel's back and made her shoot him!"

Joe sighed. "People have been shot for lesser things. Anyway, I'll get back to my guys, but I don't think we'll find anything here."

"Tire tracks," I said, "would be useful."

He gave me the thumbs-up and went back toward the pier. Dehan and I started walking back toward the car. I gave Dehan the keys, pulled on my latex gloves, and started looking at the phone. I spoke as we walked.

"The password has been disabled. The intention was clearly for the phone to be found and scrutinized."

"Has it got Telegram?"

I smiled at her. "No, and I am just looking through his WhatsApp and his text messages; they have all been deleted. So has his address book. There is absolutely nothing on the phone . . ."

We had arrived at the car, and she screwed up her face as she unlocked it. "So it was just a beacon to lead us to his body?"

I climbed in the passenger side. She got in behind the wheel, adjusted the seat, and started the engine. As she pulled away, I said, "No. There is one document, in Docs. It's addressed to me."

I read in silence for a while. Dehan glanced at me a couple of times and I started reading aloud.

"It says: 'Hey, Detective Stone, dude, you know I have always been straight with you. I know I bin'—spelled B-I-N—'I know I bin a bit of a clown, but the words I said have always been true words. Like I told you before, my daddy was a man of God who always eschewed violence, and sought the path of peace and dialogue. When I came to New York, he warned me and told me to mind I walked the straight path of righteousness. But I have strayed from that path into evil and wicked ways. I know there is no forgiveness for me, and the only thing that lies ahead is damnation and punishment, for I have committed the worst of sins, and I have taken a human life.

"'I have decided tonight to add one more sin to those I have committed already, and take my own life. I know the Lord considers suicide almost as bad as murder, for it is for Him to decide who lives and who dies, and for us to live in humble, Christian resignation of the trials which He sees fit to visit upon us, but I figure I may as well be hung for lamb as for mutton.

"'You will think that the way I am writing is strange, considering how you have heard me speak, but I may tell you that this is my true voice, the way I was raised, and not one of the fake voices which I have adopted along the way. I speak to you now in truth, and not in falsehood, as I have before.

"'I cannot delay the moment any longer. I must go and meet my Maker, and face whatever judgment He sees fit to pass on me. It is time to confess. I have committed murder, Detective Stone. I killed Dr. Robles. I shot him. My reason was a simple one. Though we had agreed to work as partners and develop the Robles-Americano electric motor, he stole my research and my ideas and then tried to cut me out. So I worked out a plan. I asked Agnes if she would reason with him on my behalf. She was always so sweet. She said she would, even though she knew it meant he'd lay into her—verbally, not physically.

"'I suggested I could come to her house and she should invite him over on some pretext. He wouldn't know I was there until he arrived. Then, between us, we could try and persuade him to reconsider his decision. I told her she could pressure him from a moral stance, appealing to his better nature, and I would cajole him with hints at a possible legal action against him.

"'But they were just excuses. I had no intention of trying to persuade him to do anything. I took my Sig along with me, and when he was sitting comfortably in his chair, enjoying his wine, I shot him. I am afraid I went crazy. I didn't even aim, Detective Stone. I just filled him full of lead, cowboy style.

"'Poor, sweet Agnes was terrified. I hated having to do it, because I was fond of Agnes, but I had to strangle her where she sat in her chair. She is now at the bottom of the East River. I only hope the good Lord took mercy on her and she is now at peace at last. I took Jose's keys and went to his house, where I retrieved the work we had done together, and which rightfully belonged to me. Then I set the scene, so it would look like Agnes had killed Jose in a jealous rage because of his affair with Alicia. It would then just be up to me to graduate with a good degree, and launch the Americano electric motor on my own.

"'That was my plan. But when you confronted me at college the other day, I knew I had no way out and it was just a matter of time before you realized what had really happened. Hats off to you. You are not an easy man to fool.

"'My time is up. Do you believe in reincarnation, Detective Stone? I do. Better luck next time. Yours, most sincerely, Americano Nielsen.'"

I flipped back to the beginning. Dehan drove in absolute silence. I read it through again twice. Then I put the phone back in the evidence bag, sealed it, and put it in my pocket.

Eventually we pulled into Fteley Avenue and Dehan parked outside the main entrance to the station. She killed the engine, the windshield wipers died, and we sat for a while, she staring at the steering wheel while I stared unseeing at the trees in front of us and made a movie in my head of everything that had happened from beginning to end.

Suddenly, Dehan took a deep breath and turned to look at me. She said, "Well, we didn't see that coming!"

I blinked, returned from my mental movie, and frowned. "Which bit?"

"That it was Am who shot Robles! I would have sworn it was Agnes. I would have sworn Dr. Meigh had her hidden somewhere. I would not in a million years have pegged Nielsen as the killer."

"Oh no," I said, "I knew it was Am who shot him. It had to be. What surprised me was the suicide note, and the phony cowboy speak. He was from Colorado. It should have come naturally to him."

THIRTEEN

Her cheeks, which were already pink from the cold, flamed red. She wrenched the hat from her head and glared at me. "No!" she said. "No! No! *No!* You did not know. You are lying!"

I shook my head. "It had to be. Who else would have had a gun like that? He told us the first time we met him. No, it was always going to be Am Nielsen."

I opened the car door and climbed out. She got out the other side and flakes of sleet began to settle on her head. She slammed the door. "Why didn't you say so?"

I shrugged. "Because it wasn't proven, and I thought your theories were brilliant and worth exploring."

I started across the road, and she fell into step with me. "You thought they were brilliant? Seriously?"

"I did. The only thing you never quite nailed was how she got the gun. For that you had to come back to Am Nielsen, which left the door open. If he provided the gun, wasn't it more logical that he shot him? He had a better potential motive than Agnes, the temperament for it, and then there was that first shot, straight to the heart. Occam's razor, remember."

"*Entia non sunt multiplicanda praeter necesitatem.*"

"That is so hot when you do that."

"Stop it."

"I always had trouble imagining the Agnes that had been described to us pulling a gun, even in jealousy. But I had no trouble at all visualizing Am shooting somebody. He was what you might describe as morally ambiguous."

"You might describe him that way. I'd describe him as an asshole."

We climbed the steps and made our way to the detectives' room. On the way, I stopped at the desk.

"Maria, did Mohamed turn up to make a statement?"

"Sure did, lover boy. Gomez took his statement."

I thanked her and followed Dehan. She dropped into her chair and threw her hat and her gloves on the desk. I sat, with the movie still playing in my head. She watched me a moment, chewing her lip.

"We got Mohamed's statement."

She continued to bite her lip a moment, then said, "So where the hell does this leave us, Stone?"

I nodded at her as though she'd said something I agreed with, then pulled over the file and looked through the photographs. When I'd finished, I pushed them over to her, took out my cell, and called Joe.

"Yeah, Stone. We didn't find anything down here. We got some partial tire tracks. We're making casts of them now, but I don't hold out much hope. What can I do for you?"

"My money is on a Land Rover."

"You are such a dude. If they are, you have to buy me a bottle of Scotch."

"Listen, do me a favor, will you? Check the Sig again for partials, however small. I want to know if Am Nielsen—the guy we just pulled from the river—I want to know if he fired the gun, then wiped it and pressed Agnes' hand onto it. I know it's a tall order, but just see if there are any wiped partials on the gun."

"I'll have a look, but it won't be anything you can take to court."

"It's more for my own curiosity, Joe, to confirm or deny a theory."

"Okay."

"And I'm sending his phone over to you. He wiped everything but his suicide note. See what you can retrieve, and get me the prints off the screen. I want to know the last person who typed on it."

"Gotcha. Hang loose."

"Yeah, you too, Joe."

I hung up and sent the file to the printer, which started to churn out pages. Dehan was sulking. "I need a holiday in Goa."

I grinned. "You wanna Goa again?"

"That's not even a joke, Stone. It's a dinosaur joke."

I shook my head. "No, this is a dinosaur joke. How do you ask a dinosaur to supper?"

"Oh Lord, no!"

"Tea, Rex?"

"Oh Lord, please, no."

"Why can't you hear a pterodactyl using the bathroom?"

"Oh good grief!"

"Because the *p* is silent."

She laughed in spite of herself and threw her hat at me. Then she became serious. "You don't believe his note, do you?"

"That's putting it a mite strongly. But there are one or two things that still trouble me."

"Like what?"

"Like the wine."

"What is it with the wine? You've been fixating on the wine since the beginning."

"He was a wine snob. More precisely, he was a Spanish wine snob."

"We established that. That's why he didn't drink the wine."

"Correct, but there are two inconsistencies here. One is that

Agnes knew that he was a Spanish wine snob, and she would not have provided California wine. Every bottle of wine in her kitchen was Spanish."

"So Am brought it with him, as an offering."

"And what do you think Agnes would have said when she saw it? If he wants to ingratiate himself with Jose Robles, bringing the wrong wine is not the best way to do it, and she would have told him that."

She made a face. "Okay, that is odd."

"But odder still is that." I pointed at the photographs. "Look at his glass."

She picked up the picture of Robles in his chair and squinted at it. "Son of a gun . . . ! The glass is almost empty."

"Look at her glass."

"A little more, but not much."

"Now look at the bottle."

"Son of a bitch! It's two-thirds empty."

"So who's been drinking the wine?"

"What does it mean? There was somebody else there? But why would somebody else drink their wine, Stone? It doesn't make sense."

"No, it doesn't make sense."

The internal phone rang. Dehan snatched it up, nodded a couple of times, and said, "Yes, sir, we'll be right up." She hung up. "The chief wants us to put him up to speed. Varoufakis is there."

"He's there, already?"

"Uh-huh."

"Boy's keen."

I picked up the printed copies of Am Nielsen's message to me and we climbed the stairs. The inspector's door was open. Dehan knocked and we went in. The assistant DA was seated opposite the inspector at his desk and stood as we entered. He was smiling a little too hard.

"Detectives! You certainly move fast. It seems it was just a few hours ago!"

I shook his proffered hand and said, "It was."

The inspector was also on his feet, gesturing at chairs. "Please, close the door and sit, and tell us what's been happening." As we sat, he added, "I don't have to say that, until we have assessed the evidence and come to some kind of determination, whatever we discuss in this room is utterly confidential."

I raised an eyebrow at him. "No, sir, you don't need to say that." I looked at Varoufakis. "We are well aware of the sensitive nature of the case, sir, but I am still very far from clear as to what is relevant evidence and what is not."

The ADA nodded. "Why don't we assess it as we go along, John? Believe me when I tell you that I am not sure myself, as yet."

Dehan leaned forward in her chair, with her elbows on her knees. "We went to the Dare 2 Dream club last night. There we met a guy who goes by the name of Mohamed, but whose real name is Daniel Brand. He was Dr. Jose Robles' lover. Apparently they were quite serious, until Robles met you, sir, and you started your relationship. Then he broke up with Brand. Brand remembered you and identified you from a photograph."

The inspector half stood. "You showed him a *photograph* of the assistant district *attorney*?"

I nodded. "Of course I did. There were no identifying features, except his face." I turned to Costas. "Brand recognized you, sir, from dancing with Robles."

He seemed to sag into his chair. "It wasn't my finest hour, Detectives."

I shrugged. "It's not an issue, sir. But you need to decide whether you want to keep it secret or not. As long as you keep it secret but continue to go to clubs like the Dare 2 Dream, you are at risk, and your professional integrity is compromised because you expose yourself to blackmail."

Varoufakis nodded again. He looked sick. "You are right, of

course, but I am married, John, and I have two young children. The Greek community is not the most tolerant on this issue."

Dehan sighed. "Brand was here this morning, shortly after ten. He made a statement."

The inspector looked mad and flopped back in his chair, eyeing the assistant DA. "Which brings us to the events of this morning."

I handed them each a copy of Am's suicide note and let them read it. When he'd finished, the ADA said, "This is a confession."

I gave my head a slight sideways jerk that said it was and it wasn't. "Technically it's a confession because he says he killed Dr. Robles. It is on his phone, but it is not signed by him. We're checking to see who the last person was who typed on that screen. Whether it is a true confession is still a moot point."

He frowned. "What do you mean? You have reason to doubt the veracity of it?"

"I'm not satisfied. There are a number of things about it that worry me."

The inspector scratched his chin. "Like what, John?"

"Small things that could be significant: for a start, his language."

He narrowed his eyes. "His *language*?"

Dehan answered. "Am was a self-confessed clown. He used to adopt different personas. When he first called us, he adopted the persona of a black gangster from the Bronx, but when we went to see him, he claimed to be from Colorado and he acted the part of a Colorado redneck trying to integrate into the Bronx black community. He was a very complex character, sir. When we surprised him with his friends, at the university, his speech was perfectly normal, and so was his behavior. However, Stone thinks, and I agree, that the language in the note is affectedly redneck. It's not authentic."

Varoufakis burst out laughing. "That is hardly reason to dismiss his confession, Detectives!"

I said, "That is just one thing. The other is the wine. It seems to me the glasses of wine were staged. The lab tells us neither Robles nor Agnes drank from their glasses, yet both glasses have only a small amount of wine in them, and the bottle is only a third full. Yet Robles had contempt for American wine, and Agnes knew this. She would not have given him California wine. The wine in her house and in his house is all Spanish. She was at pains to please him. Nor would she have allowed Nielsen to give him California wine if she was trying to help him win Robles over. So what is that wine doing there—and who drank it?"

The assistant DA sighed heavily. "Okay, knowing Jose quite well, I can confirm that he did consider California wine beneath contempt and would not have drunk it. But it was an affectation. He played the arrogant, aggressive control freak, but underneath he was actually a kind, humane person. It is entirely possible that Nielsen brought a bottle with him, and Jose sniffed it and refused to drink it while Nielsen and Agnes drank a glass each. After shooting Jose, he would have washed his own glass and, as he said, set the scene to frame Agnes."

I nodded. "Yes, that is an explanation, but it's not what happened."

"Excuse me? Based on what?"

"Based on my knowledge of the characters involved."

"I think I know Jose somewhat better than you do, Detective!"

"Yes, and your view is subjective and your judgment biased. Agnes would not have allowed Dr. Robles even to see that bottle. If she called him to come to her house, at that time of night, to intercede on Am's behalf, she would have had a bottle of Rioja or Ribera del Duero Reserva or Gran Reserva. I saw bottles of both in her kitchen. It makes no sense that she would allow that bottle of California wine to be served."

He shook his head and his eyes were bright. "It's absurd."

I looked at the inspector. "I'm sorry, sir. Mr. Varoufakis has a vested interest in having this case closed without his relationship to Dr. Robles becoming public knowledge, and if I can avoid that,

I will. But I am not going to close a case on the strength of an unsigned confession which I believe to be unsafe." I looked Varoufakis in the eye and added, "I also think that your relationship with Dr. Robles gives you a conflict of interest and you should not be involved in this investigation."

"I was the one who pressed for this investigation, for God's sake!"

"Yes, and now you need to distance yourself from it, sir."

The ADA was about to reply, but the inspector cut across him. "They're right, Costas. You know yourself that they are. We will do our level best to keep your name out of it, but this is a murder investigation, and we have to follow the evidence—wherever it leads."

He was quiet for a long while then looked at me, and his eyes were angry. "You *have* a confession!"

"I have a confession I believe to be unsafe. And frankly, Costas, you should have come clean about your involvement from the start."

He stood and moved to the door. Dehan stopped him. "Mr. Varoufakis?"

He turned. "What is it, Detective?"

"You're asking us for latitude and understanding, to bend the rules for you, but I want to ask you something. If a colleague of yours had done what you have done, only with a woman instead of a man, would you expect us to be understanding and give him latitude?" He stared at her but didn't answer. She narrowed her eyes and shook her head. "A man who cheats on his wife is a rat and deserves what he gets, it makes no difference if he cheats with a man or a woman. If you have kids, that makes you twice the rat because you're risking their happiness and their well-being too. Go home to your wife and kids and pray your affair isn't relevant to the investigation. And while you're about it, grow up. You're a big boy now."

He left and closed the door behind him. We were quiet for a

moment, then Dehan shrugged. "I got no time for cheats. You make a commitment, you stand by it. End of story."

"Indeed." The inspector nodded. "I can't argue with you on that. But where does this leave us? Are you serious about this confession? You know I'll back you up whatever you decide, but I have to agree with Costas, you *have* a confession, and your doubts seem to be founded on some pretty slim evidence. The wine and the language . . . Both may have perfectly simple explanations."

I nodded. "Oh, I agree, sir, we could probably come up with a number of explanations, but they would not satisfy Occam's razor. They would not be the most simple answers. We would be making the evidence fit the answer, not the other way around."

"Well, what *is* the most simple explanation, if not that the confession is true? Either Agnes Shine killed him, and for some reason this Am Nielsen is confessing to the crime, or the confession is true, and Dr. Shine is dead too. It has to be one or the other, surely!"

Dehan nodded. "I agree. Besides, Stone, you said yourself in the car that you knew Am Nielsen had shot Robles. I am getting pretty confused about what you think happened here."

I shook my head. "No, the most simple explanation is that Am Nielsen shot Dr. Robles, but Agnes Shine was not there to advise him about the wine." I looked at them both in turn and smiled. "We need to find Agnes Shine."

FOURTEEN

The deputy inspector's eyes had glazed over, and he had nodded a few times as though he had some idea of what I was talking about. Finally, he'd told us to carry on, we were doing a fine job, and to keep him posted. We had left him shaking his head at the cold, gray window, and Dehan had followed me downstairs with the wooden motions of a string puppet, staring at her feet as she took each step. We had sat at the desk, and she had watched me pick up the phone and call Dr. Patricia Meigh, with a small frown on her forehead.

"Dr. Meigh, this is Detective John Stone."

"Good afternoon, Detective, how can I help you? I hope you found what you were looking for the other day, or not, as the case may be."

"Thank you," I said, somewhat ambiguously. "Things have moved on a little since then."

"Are you any closer to identifying Jose's killer?"

"Oh, yes, indeed we are, but there are a few things which I am not one hundred percent clear about, Dr. Meigh. I was wondering if you would be willing to come in before you head off for Maine, and just tidy up a few loose ends for us."

"Of course, Detective. I would be happy to. When would suit you?"

"Could you manage it this afternoon?"

"In about an hour?"

I made a "well, that's surprising" face at Dehan and said, "An hour would be superb. Thank you, Dr. Meigh."

Dehan said, "She is very cooperative," and sounded worried. "Are you sure you're on the right track?"

"No."

"You're not?"

"No, because I don't know what track I am on. I am just following the inconsistencies."

"Yeah, you say that, and then you say"—she put on an absurd male voice—"'Oh, yeah, well, I knew all along that Am shot him, that was obvious!'"

I smiled. "Well, it was kind of obvious, you must admit. But I didn't know why and I still don't. Just as I am convinced Agnes was not there when Am killed Robles, but I don't know why, or where she was."

"So how can Meigh help?"

"I think there's an at least even chance she knows where Agnes is."

"So there is *something* in my theory?"

"I told you, it was a brilliant theory, Dehan."

Today was my day for being subtly ambiguous.

Forty-five minutes later, Dr. Meigh showed up in a gleaming white Audi and was shown up to interview room one. We followed a couple of minutes later. She was sitting at the table in a pale blue suit with a white blouse and a string of pearls around her neck. She had a dark blue cashmere coat folded on the table. Her hair was carelessly perfect, and she smiled as we came in. I was struck again by how large her presence was, considering how petite she was.

Dehan returned the smile and said, "It is very good of you to come in, Dr. Meigh. We know how busy you are."

"I am happy to help."

We sat, and I leaned my elbows on the table. "Dr. Meigh, let me come straight to the point. Where is Agnes Shine?"

Her eyebrows shot up, but she didn't lose her smile or her cool. "I have no idea! What on Earth makes you think I know?"

"Because you lied to us about how close you were."

"I certainly did not."

"You led us to believe that you were little more than acquaintances, Dr. Meigh . . ."

"I believe what I said was that she was as close to me as she was to anybody, except Jose. And that is true."

"Which was actually a misleading answer. We asked you how close you were, but you didn't mention that she went to stay with you every weekend."

"Why should I? I don't see how that is remotely relevant."

"Is that where she is now?"

"Don't be absurd!"

I sat back, and Dehan frowned. "In what way exactly is that absurd, Dr. Meigh?"

"Do you really think I would risk my career and my position at the university by harboring a fugitive from the law?"

Dehan's frown deepened. "I don't know. Would you?"

"Of course not! Look here, is this what this interview is going to consist of? You bullying me about my friendship with Agnes?"

I smiled amiably. "No. You were friends then? More than simply acquaintances?"

"Yes, of course we were."

"Had she told you about Dr. Robles' visits to the Dare 2 Dream club?"

She hesitated. "She hinted that his attraction for Alicia was possibly a front."

"And what about Am Nielsen?"

"What about him?"

"You were initially against his joining Dr. Robles' research team."

"Well, he was a bit of a clown."

"You told us you didn't know who he was."

"You reminded me, and I refreshed my memory. As I say, he was a clown."

"But he proved to be an asset in the end."

"He was a good student, and Jose seemed to like him. Jose was effectively leading the research; it was his choice of team."

"They were close."

"Quite close, yes."

"Do you think they were lovers?"

She looked genuinely startled. "Good heavens, no!"

"You seem very certain."

"Well, it just never occurred to me . . ."

"Dr. Meigh, where is the missing part of Dr. Robles' research?"

"What?"

"What you showed us the other day was incomplete. The developments he was working on with Am Nielsen were not there."

"How could you *possibly* know that?"

"Where is the rest of his research?"

"What I showed you is everything we have. There is nothing else."

I sighed and drummed my fingers on the table for a moment. "You described Dr. Robles as brilliant. You described both him and Agnes as brilliant."

"They were. I hope she still is."

"Yet what you showed us at your house was nothing but a very pedestrian review of existing technology. That is not exactly what you could describe as brilliant."

Her cheeks colored. She drew breath, hesitated, and looked away. "Look, Detective, I am a scientist, but my position at the university means that most of my work is administrative. You might even say political. I represent the interests of the university. I deal a lot with Washington and major industrial interests. I quite simply have no time for actual research. So I delegate it. My team's published work will credit Dr. Patricia Meigh *et al*. But the truth is it is the *et al.* who do the actual scientific investigation. I employ people like Dr. Robles, they benefit from the university's reputation and financial clout, and I benefit from their brilliance."

I nodded. "You're an academic. Your interest is in the corner office."

"That is a little uncharitable, but yes, essentially that is how it works. My point is I have not actually examined Jose's work in some time. I know in general terms what it is about and what it aims to achieve, but I have not reviewed it for several months. We were due to go over it in January, in fact."

I grunted. "Well, if I were you, I would review it a damn sight sooner than that, because all the key developments are missing."

I waited for her to say something, but she just stared at me. Dehan said, "While we are on the subject, Dr. Meigh, perhaps you could explain something to me."

Meigh's eyes shifted. She was beginning to look alarmed. "What?"

"If you are not personally involved in the research, why was it at your house? Why wasn't it at the university, or at Dr. Robles' house?"

She closed her eyes and sighed. "You are determined to see me as a villain in all this, and you are going to pick on every tiny irregularity."

Dehan shook her head. "Not at all, we are just asking you to explain. Can you?"

"Yes, of course I can. I just told you we were planning a review of the team's work in January, immediately after Christmas."

I said, "When you got back from Maine."

"Yes. I was planning a get-together with the team for a long weekend. We would eat, drink, discuss the work, and do a bit of brainstorming. Science is a creative business, and we work best in a relaxed environment like that. So we had started shipping the research over. It is entirely possible that the more advanced stuff is in electronic format at the lab in the university."

I nodded. "Then we will need to see it."

"I understand. Are we done? I would like to leave now."

"There is just one last thing, Dr. Meigh. Agnes has disappeared without a trace. I am quite certain that she was not murdered along with Dr. Robles. Now, disappearing that thoroughly requires a lot of skill. It requires the skills of a trained agent, and even they don't always manage it. It requires things like fake ID documents: Social Security number, driver's license . . . In a word, it requires field craft. You and I both know that Agnes Shine does not have field craft. And that means that somebody is sheltering her. There is only one person that can be. So you need to give some very careful thought to what you do next, Dr. Meigh, because what started out as a desire to help a friend in trouble could end up becoming accessory to murder, or, if the DA feels you didn't cooperate when you should have, conspiracy to murder. Either way, you are looking at serious time. Think it over, and call me."

Her cheeks were burning. She stood, snatched her coat, and slammed out of the room. Dehan stood and walked across the room till she was two inches from the wall, with her hands stuffed in her back pockets. "Stone, I hate to say it, and I have not exactly shone in this case so far, but I believe her."

"None of us has shone in this case, Dehan. This case is like wading through mangroves at midnight with no moon and sunglasses on. She is very credible. I'm inclined to believe her myself. Come on, let's go do some homework."

She turned to face me. "Homework?"

"Yeah, old-fashioned wading through files, eliminating the impossible, checking registers . . . that kind of stuff. I want you to find out what Meigh's husband does for a living."

"Yay. Wait, can we go to Goa instead?"

We went downstairs and spent the next two hours going through births, deaths, marriages, company directories, and the land registry. It was slow, tedious, and largely unrewarding work. The light was starting to fade outside when my phone rang. The number was withheld.

"Yeah, Detective Stone."

"Detective Stone, I would like to meet with you, to discuss the Am Nielsen murder." The voice was pleasant, even cultured.

"Who am I speaking to?" I waved at Dehan and mouthed, *Get a trace.*

"I'm not going to tell you, Detective. And I am not going to stay on long enough for you to have the call traced."

"I need to know at least . . ."

"All you need to know, Detective, is that I will meet you in an hour at the park gates opposite the Bronx Zoo. Come alone. If there is anybody with you, I won't show. I have information you need."

He hung up. Dehan had the other receiver in her hand and shook her head. "Not a chance. Who was it?"

"A guy who wants to meet me alone, park entrance opposite the Bronx Zoo. Says he has information about Am Nielsen's murder."

"You can't go alone, Stone."

"I can't afford not to. We're at a dead end, Dehan."

"You think so?" She looked doubtful.

I smiled and shook my head. "No, but I do think this is the breakthrough we need, and we can't afford to blow it." I pointed at her computer. "Did you find anything?"

She nodded. "I think it could be significant."

"Tell me."

She filled me in on what she had found, and bit by bit, the mangrove started to make sense to me. The only problem was, everything was circumstantial; everything was a theory. And Am Nielsen's killer knew that. As things stood, there was no way of proving a goddamn thing. Dehan looked up at me and shrugged. "What does any of this prove, Stone? I can see by your face that this is what you were looking for, but I have no idea why."

"I can't explain right now, it just confirms some thoughts I had. It's beginning to make sense. Some of it, at least."

"So share!"

"I have to go."

She sighed. "You should take backup."

I shook my head. "He might get spooked."

"Wear a wire at least."

I thought about it. "Okay, I'll call you when I get there and leave my cell on. You can listen in. Will that do?"

She didn't look happy. "Okay, but don't get hurt anywhere important. You still owe me five kids."

"Five? Last week it was seven, what happened?"

"I'm serious."

"I'll call you when I get there."

I had left with plenty of time. It's less than a three-mile drive from the station house to the zoo, but at that time of the evening the traffic was heavy going out of town, and the dark and the sleet made the progress slow. Besides which, I'd wanted to get there early, so I could see him arrive.

I took the Bronx River Parkway going north and came off at the Fordham Road exit, followed the loop around, crossed the bridge, and found the entrance to the park on my right. There I pulled in, killed the engine and the lights, took my phone out of my pocket, and settled down to wait.

I waited fifteen minutes. My feet were going numb, and I was thinking about getting out of the car to stamp around for a bit when the cab was flooded by light and a large, dark Land Rover pulled in past me. It moved up to the gate, did a three-point turn so it was facing me, killed the lights and the engine, and waited.

I pressed Call on my phone, put it in my pocket, and got out of the car. It was dark, but there was enough light from Fordham Road for me to see the driver's window slide down. Through it I could see a dark gray coat sleeve, but nothing else. I approached a few steps, and the same voice I'd heard on the phone said, "That's close enough."

"What do you want?"

"I have a message for you, Detective. You and your partner are out of your depth. You need to back off and close this investigation."

I gave a small, rather humorless laugh. "Get real, pal."

"It's you who needs to get real, Stone. There are big interests involved here, you are just a pawn. Now, I am going to do you a favor, and you had better accept it. Am Nielsen killed Dr. Robles. You have his confession. Close the case."

I shook my head. "First of all, who is this message from? Second, what motive did Am have? Third, where is Agnes Shine? I know for a fact he didn't kill her."

He was silent for a moment, like he was thinking about the questions.

"Dr. Robles was going to sell his research, and Am's, to the LightYear Corporation. Am found out and killed him."

"How do you know? Who is this message from?"

"Enough questions, Detective."

"What about Agnes?"

"Agnes Shine is dead."

"Who killed her?"

"She did. The case is closed, Detective Stone."

"I need proof."

"No. You don't. You have a confession. I told you, you are out of your depth. This no longer concerns the NYPD. Now, take your wife, go to Goa, and close the case. Otherwise you'll be attending her funeral instead."

The window slid up, the engine rumbled to life, and the big truck pulled out onto Fordham Road, where it disappeared west into the city.

I stood for a moment looking at the amber-washed blacktop, with its sporadic stream of cars. Then I walked back to my Jag and leaned on the roof, thinking. My teeth were beginning to chatter with the cold, but all I could think of was his last words.

A car approaching from the east began to indicate right. It

slowed and pulled in beside the Jag. The door opened and Dehan got out, in her woolen hat and gloves.

I smiled at her. "I should have known."

"The inspector is looking into the LightYear Corporation now. Who was that guy? Did you get his registration?"

"Yeah, but two gets you twenty they were fake, magnetic plates. He tried to imply he was from some kind of government agency. But that was bullshit."

I put my arms around her and held her for a moment. She gave me a squeeze and I kissed her hat. "Come on, Bombur, let's get back to the station and have a chat with the chief."

She looked up at me. "Bombur?"

"Yeah, you know, Bofur's brother."

I kissed her nose and climbed in the Jag.

FIFTEEN

We sat in the deputy inspector's office listening to the recording Dehan had made of the conversation. When it had finished, he grunted and leaned back in his chair.

"No longer concerns the NYPD? Out of your depth? And Detective Dehan's funeral." He turned to consider me. "Did you recognize him?"

I shook my head. "No, but there aren't that many people it could be. I can only think of two, and one of those is very unlikely."

"I agree. Carmen?"

"One thing struck me, sir. The repetition, twice, of the phrase, 'You have a confession.' We've heard that before, very recently. Also, he knew I wanted to go to Goa. We need to think who's heard me mention that."

He nodded. "I was thinking the same thing. Costas. It's a shame. He's a good man, but it's a slippery slope. It starts with what seems to be a harmless lie, and before you know it..."

The silence was more eloquent than any words he could have used. I said, "We can't prove it was Costas, sir. Did you turn anything up on the LightYear Corporation?"

"Not much so far. Started small in San Francisco. Very aggressive. Expanded quickly. Their thing seems to be launching cutting-edge, innovative technology. They have expressed an interest in collaborating with companies like Tesla."

Dehan shrugged. "But any approach they made to Robles would have been untraceable and a hundred percent deniable by the company."

I scratched my head. "But let's assume that it's true. It is certainly credible. Let's assume that the LightYear Corporation approach Robles and make him an offer for his research, which, as we know, legally belongs to the university, and which morally belongs partly to Am Nielsen. The first question is, how did Am learn about Robles' planned sellout? The only people who would know about it would be Robles himself and LightYear."

Dehan shook her head. "Unless he told Costas? He might have consulted Costas as to the legal implications, trying to cover his back."

I nodded. "Okay, so that means that Costas then informed Am? What purpose could he have for doing that? We still draw a blank there. And here is another blank. What motive has anyone got for murdering Am?"

The inspector frowned at me. "Surely that was suicide, John?"

"No. The more I think about it, the more certain I am that he was murdered. And I'm pretty sure I can prove it. First of all, there was the phrasing of the letter. It was unnatural, like somebody trying to write like a redneck and not knowing how. Second, drowning yourself is probably the most difficult way to commit suicide. The reflex against inhaling water is just too powerful. He was young, strong, and fit; there was no way he was going to drown in ten or fifteen feet of water in a small bay six or seven feet from the pier. That just isn't credible." I pulled out my phone and called Frank.

"Stone, what a surprise."

I put it on speaker. "Listen, Frank, this is important."

"More surprises."

"I mean it. Did Am Nielsen have bruising on his lower arms and wrists?"

"You know he did."

"So the water in his lungs, I need you to . . ."

"I'm looking at the initial results right here, John. I know my job. I can't tell you yet what kind of water it is, but I can tell you it's not saline, which it would have been if he had drowned in the Harlem, it being tidal. He was drowned somewhere else, in clear water. And yes, the bruises are consistent with having had his arms held behind his back. He also has bruising to his scalp, where his head was held down." He paused. "By the way, Robles' last meal was Scotch whiskey."

"Yeah, I kind of knew that. Thanks, Frank. You're one of a kind." I hung up and looked at them. "Somebody used Am to kill Robles."

Dehan said, "Costas." She looked at us both in turn. "It makes perfect sense. Robles' big obsession was dominating people and hurting them, right? He was a sadist and a bully. He used Costas to hurt Mohamed—Daniel Brand—and once he had Costas hooked, he went for him, started threatening to blow the whistle on him. We can't prove it yet, but it is a pretty safe bet. Then, when Robles consults him about the offer from LightYear, Costas sees his chance. He tells Am about it, convinces him the only way to save his work is to kill Robles. Maybe he even suggests selling the research to LightYear as his own, who knows? Point is, the plan is to frame Agnes as the jealous lover. So Costas gets Agnes out of the house for the night on some pretext, calls Robles to come over, badabim badabam badaboom, they kill him and frame her. And remember, Costas himself told us he knew nothing about wine."

The inspector nodded. "Then he pressed me to investigate, partly to cover himself but also partly in the hope of casting suspicion on Agnes, whom they had framed. But when the investigation went too deep, he killed Am and planted the partially true confession on him. I imagine the muscle who carried out the actual killing was the same man in the car. I can't see Costas doing it himself." He thought for a moment. "How do you want to proceed? We pull in Costas and force a confession out of him?"

I shook my head. "We haven't much leverage yet. Frank will be looking for prints on Am's arms and scalp. We might get lucky."

I went to the window and stood looking awhile at where the sleet had turned to soft flakes and was starting to drift on the sidewalks under the yellow light of the streetlamps.

"The key to this whole thing is that research." I turned to look at them where they were both watching me, Dehan uncertain and the inspector frowning, curious.

"Whatever the motive for Robles' killing, that research played a central role. I want to go to Costas and tell him we are closing the case, and to rest easy. Then I want a twenty-four-hour-a-day watch on him. If he has that research, he is going to try and sell it.

"Meanwhile, we get a warrant. We go to Dr. Meigh and we tell her the murder aspect of the case is closed, but we need to tidy up the issue of the research, which appears to have been stolen. We search her house and the team's offices and computers at the university. If it shows up . . ." I shrugged. "We conclude she was telling the truth. If it doesn't . . ."

Dehan interrupted. "If it doesn't, we need to give Costas a choice: confess and save his family public humiliation, or drag them through a trial."

The inspector nodded. "I agree. Costas is our man. Fine, good work as always. I'll apply for the warrant first thing in the morning. Now I suggest you two get home and get some rest."

We went down, grabbed our coats, and made our way out to the car. I climbed behind the wheel, and she sat next to me, watching me as I stared out at the trees in the parking lot in front of me.

"You going to start the car or are you going to freeze us to death instead?"

I turned the key and the engine roared. I backed out and headed for the boulevard.

"So," I said, "if someday we decided to have kids . . ."

"What do you mean, 'if'? That's decided. It's going to happen."

"Okay, when we decide to have kids . . ."

"Will I continue to work? I don't know, Stone. I'm old school. Happiest, healthiest kid is the one who has his mom at home. Home smells of baking. You know what I mean? There are probably a thousand psychologists and sociologists out there who can prove I'm wrong. But what the hell do they know? They're probably all screwed up because their mothers were out burning bras and smoking hash instead of baking cakes at home."

"And I'm the dinosaur?"

"Hey! Don't knock the dinosaurs."

"I'm serious, Dehan. This guy threatened to kill you tonight."

She gave a short, adolescent laugh. "But he threatened to kill me because *you* are a cop!"

"Well, yes, that's true. But the point is, being a cop in the Bronx is dangerous."

We were quiet for a while, looking at the illuminated shop fronts and the Christmas decorations reflecting off the sidewalks, sidewalks that were slowly turning white under the gathering snow.

"You're right. It's something we need to think about. Both of us. A kid needs her father as much as she needs her mother. And when you lose your dad, it hurts just as much. I know all about that."

We drove the rest of the way in silence. My mind kept going back to the dark Land Rover, the heavy coat and the arm and shoulder just visible in the limpid light, the voice pleasant, educated. "This no longer concerns the NYPD. Now, take your wife, go to Goa, and close the case. Otherwise you'll be attending her funeral instead."

There was something jarring about the chauvinistic phrasing: take your wife to Goa, as though she could not afford to go herself. I had told the inspector I did not recognize the man, and I didn't, not personally, but the more I thought about him, the more familiar his manner seemed: his manner and his style.

I pulled up outside our house, killed the engine and the lights, and climbed out. The road was silent. Patchy snow had accumulated on the sidewalk and banked up against the walls and fences. Lamplight filtered through the naked branches of the plane trees. Dehan climbed out and her boots crunched on the snow on the sidewalk. Her door slammed, and she smiled at me from under her brown-and-white woolen hat.

"Dehan," I said, "let me always remember you just like that."

Down the road, a car door clunked. Dehan began to walk carefully across the frozen sidewalk. "I look better in a bikini, you know."

"A guy can have more than one memory."

I followed her toward the gate. She pushed through and stopped at the first step. I looked down the road. There was a man approaching, silhouetted against the haze from the streetlamp behind him. Condensation drifted from his mouth. He was walking briskly, head down. Without thinking, I said, "Go up, Dehan, get inside."

"What is it?"

"Nothing. Just go up, open the door."

She took a step up. The man was ten paces away. I saw his right elbow jut out and snapped, "No! Don't! Get down!"

His hand was out and he was running, aiming. I heard my voice bellow, "*Get down!*"

Fire seemed to spit from his extended arm, once, twice, three times. I dropped and heard a slug smack and whine off the neighbor's steps. Another smacked into our wall under the bow window. The third showered redbrick dust over my head from the wall in front of me. By then, I had my .45 in my hand. I stood and took aim. He was already aiming at me, ten or twelve feet away. I heard Dehan scream, "*Stone! No!*"

His weapon spat a second before mine, but by then, Dehan was already colliding with me, knocking me to the ground. A searing heat in my left shoulder told me I'd been hit, but as I crashed on the sidewalk, with Dehan on top of me, I was thinking we were sitting targets. So I let off two rounds blindly in his general direction.

When I opened my eyes, it was to see his retreating form, running unsteadily on the icy sidewalk, and Dehan, in her coat, gloves, and woolly hat, hurtling after him.

I scrambled to my feet. Shards of pain pierced my winded chest, but I ignored them and took off after Dehan. Down the road, tires squealed and headlamps blinded me. I shielded my eyes and saw Dehan seem to levitate and slam her boots into the guy's back. He sprawled to the ground on his face, and she landed with one knee on his back. The car was accelerating toward her. I screamed, "*Dehan! The car!*"

I could see she had his right arm pulled back and was twisting it savagely. I could hear her shouting at him: "*Who do you work for? Who do you work for?*"

Then the car was screaming to a halt, skidding and fishtailing on the snow. Dehan was jumping, rolling for cover. A hail of bullets hit the sidewalk in her wake, lifting a mist of snow and cement dust. The guy was staggering to his feet, running for the car. I was bellowing, "*NYPD! Freeze! Freeze!*"

I emptied two rounds blindly into the vehicle. I heard a thunk of metal and the shattering of glass. The passenger door opened and the guy clambered in. Then the car hurtled away down the road.

I ran to Dehan. "Are you hurt?"

She stood. "I'm okay! You?"

"Yeah, I'm okay."

She was dialing her phone as she stepped toward me. "Detective Dehan, I want a BOLO out on a dark blue Audi A8, old model, maybe 2016, license plate G-A-something, last two numbers a six and a three. Two males, late twenties, early thirties, possibly injured. One short-haired, six foot, well built, black leather coat and blue jeans. Possible broken fingers on right hand. Both armed and very dangerous. Car has a bullet hole in front right wing and a shattered windshield. I also need a crime scene team at my house. Yeah, Haight Avenue." She hung up. "You're hit."

"It's just a graze." I laughed. "Your flying tackle did more damage than the slug."

"You are one crazy son of a bitch, Stone. You stood up in his line of fire. It's a miracle you weren't killed."

"Another two strides and he would have taken us both out. You know that. I had to stop him."

"Come on, you big brute. Let's get you inside."

Far off, I could hear the howl of sirens approaching across the night. As we walked, I said, "Did he tell you anything? You were going to break his arm. That's illegal, you know? You are not allowed to break prisoners' arms."

"I was only bluffing. I would only have dislocated his shoulder. But no, all he said was 'agh, agh.' But he wasn't wearing gloves."

"What do you mean? He would have said more if he'd had gloves on?"

She smiled as we reached the front steps and pulled a Glock 19 from her coat pocket, wrapped in a handkerchief. "Prints," she said simply. "Am I a good girl? Do you think Santa will bring me tickets to Goa this year?"

"You are some piece of work, Dehan. I am in awe."

"Awe? Really?"

She giggled. Two patrol cars turned in off Rhinelander Avenue and accelerated toward us. As we watched them pull up, she said, "He didn't give us very long, did he? Did he know we had decided not to drop the case? Has he got a source? Or was this guy only intended to scare us?"

I watched the lights pulsing red and blue on the snow and the officers climbing out and moving toward us. "Whichever way you look at it," I said, "it is not coherent."

SIXTEEN

I took the gun from Dehan and put it into an evidence bag from my pocket. Gomez and Smith were the first to get to us, closely followed by Derringer and Hoffmeier. I handed the gun to Gomez.

"Hoffmeier, you and Derringer go with Detective Dehan and cordon off the area. Find where the car was parked, cordon that off too. You never know, there might be a cigarette butt or something. Gomez, I want you to take this to the lab. I'll call ahead and tell them you're coming. If Joe is still there, you hand it to him personally. If not, whoever is standing in for him. This has to be processed tonight. Scram."

She took it, and she and Smith withdrew at speed, with the siren blaring. While Dehan returned to the scene of the fight, with Hoffmeier and Derringer, I called Joe at the lab.

"Good evening, John!"

"You still at the lab?"

"I was just putting my coat on, why?"

"Couple of guys just tried to pop me and Dehan with a Glock 19."

"Oh, that was you, was it? A team is on its way. They just left."

"Yeah, Dehan managed to wrestle the piece out of the shooter's hand."

Joe burst out laughing. "She's one in a million!"

"No argument from me. She probably saved my life. Anyway, the gun is on its way to the lab right now in a patrol car. Sergeant Gomez has it. There's a BOLO out on the shooters and their vehicle..."

"And you'd like the prints to go with it. I'll do it myself, John, and run them. I'll let you know the moment we get a match."

"I appreciate that, Joe. Thanks."

I hung up and called the inspector.

"John, good evening, what can I do for you?"

"I'm sorry to disturb you at home, sir." He muttered something about "not at all" and I went on, "Two men just tried to shoot us outside our front door."

"Good heavens, man! Are you all right? And Carmen?"

"Yes, we're fine, thank you, sir. She managed to get most of the registration of the car, I put two rounds into it, and there is a BOLO out. Dehan also managed to wrestle the gun from the shooter's hand. She may have broken his fingers in the process. His prints are being run as we speak."

"That girl is something, isn't she!"

"Yes, sir. Now, here's the thing. This had to be Costas, and I want him arrested right now."

"Yes, I see... How can you be so certain?"

"It can't be anybody else. It has panic written all over it, and the only person panicking right now is Costas. Simple process of elimination. He told us to drop the case and accept the confession. I said I wouldn't, and as soon as I get home there is a car waiting for me and the shooter tries to kill us both. It's Costas."

"I'll have a car sent to his house and have him brought in." He hesitated. "You are sure about this, John...?"

"One hundred percent. I'm going to have something to eat and get a few hours' sleep. I'll talk to him first thing in the morning. Have them let me know when he's in custody, will you?"

"Right, right. Of course I will. Get some rest. Good work."

The crime scene van had arrived while I was talking. Liz Greene was heading the team, and we ran through the events together, setting yellow markers where each event took place. We managed to recover most of the slugs, and she took my Colt in for comparison. We recovered the spent shells from the Glock but found nothing where the Audi had been parked. After that, there was little to do but wait for the results to come back from the lab.

When they had gone, we went inside, and Dehan tended to my shoulder. My coat, my jacket, and my shirt were ruined, and there was a channel gouged out of my upper arm, one inch long and a quarter of an inch deep. It hurt like hell, but I refused to show it, and two aspirins and a glass of Bushmills made it tolerable. At half past nine, when we were putting the dishes in the dishwasher, the phone rang.

"Detective Stone?"

"Speaking."

"This is Gomez, sir. Deputy Inspector John Newman asked me to let you know as soon as we had Assistant District Attorney Varou..."

"Varoufakis."

"Yes, sir, thank you, in custody. We have him in custody, sir, at the Forty-Third."

"Thank you, Gomez. Good work."

I hung up and looked at Dehan where she was hunkered down, pressing buttons on the dishwasher. It started to hum, and she stood.

"Varoufakis is in custody."

"Good. So it's over. Now we have a drink each, you put your good arm around me, we watch something totally mindless on TV, and then you carry me up to the bedroom."

"Sounds like barbarian heaven."

"I think so."

It didn't happen in exactly that order, but the next morning at eight, we were at the station. Costas was upstairs in interview room three, and I was on the phone talking to Liz Greene, from the lab. She was saying, "His name is Peter Yeltsin. He is wanted in Russia on several counts of murder, extortion, and drug trafficking, and he is wanted in California, Arizona, and Texas for questioning on similar matters. I hope they catch him, he's a very dangerous man."

"They found the car last night. There were bloodstains, so it looks like they're both hurt. They'll show up before long. Thanks, Liz."

I hung up. Dehan was standing, waiting. I said, "The shooter is linked to the Russian Mafia, a hard case. We were lucky."

She shook her head. "No, *you* were lucky. I was skilled." She jerked her head. "Come on, let's go talk to this son of a bitch. Apparently he has waived his right to an attorney. Inspector says the DA is on her way."

We climbed the stairs and pushed into the room. He didn't look up. He looked gray and drawn in his orange jumpsuit. We sat opposite him. Dehan went through the formalities and started recording.

I said, "You know the problem with the Russians, Costas? They are big and bold, but they are not subtle. If you want to terrorize a neighborhood, the Russians are your go-to guys. But if you want a nice, subtle job of assassination, the Israelis, the British, the Chinese, the Japanese. Efficient, tidy, get the job done and vanish. But the Russians, they'll mess it up every time."

He didn't answer. I said, "You're not wondering why I am talking to you about the Russian Mafia, Costas?" He still said nothing. "Come on, you waived your right to an attorney, you may as well speak to us."

"You haven't asked me a question yet, Detective. What do you want me to say?"

"All right, let's get to the questions. Do you know Peter Yeltsin?"

He closed his eyes and went a shade grayer. "Yes, I know him."

"Did you hire him to have us killed?"

"No."

Dehan slammed her hand down on the table. Costas leaned back. She leaned forward and yelled in his face, "*You're lying!*"

"I did not hire him to kill you! I hired him to scare you! It wasn't even my idea! It was his!"

I laughed. It wasn't a nice laugh. "Come on, Costas! You know that cuts no ice. If he had killed us, you would have been as liable for murder as he was. He attempted to murder us, and you are liable for conspiracy to murder and attempted murder."

"That was never my intention. All I wanted was to scare you into accepting Nielsen's confession. You were going to destroy my life!"

I made a face like he'd said something reasonable and I was thinking about it. "Yes, let's talk about Am Nielsen. Did you employ Yeltsin to do that job too?"

"That was suicide and you know it! You can't pin that on me!"

"Nielsen was murdered, Costas."

"What is this, your ridiculous theory about how his voice was all wrong?"

"Partly that, yes."

"So, here we go, the NYPD up to its old tricks. You've got me for trying to save my marriage and my family, after making one stupid mistake, in trying to understand my own sexuality and my gender ambiguity, and because of the rampant, homophobic, Republican prejudices of your partner, you are now out to destroy me and pin every unsolved case you can find on me! Truth and Justice, the American way! The president would be proud of you!"

Dehan looked at me, then looked at Costas. "You done?"

"Go ahead, do your worst. I slept with a man, I must be a morally twisted monster. Haven't you got some cases of cannibalism and torturing of babies you can pin on me?"

"*Now* are you done?"

"Go ahead."

"Because there is the small matter of the bruising on his arms and on the back of his head, consistent with having been held facedown, and the water in his lungs. See, he did drown, but he did not drown in the Harlem. He drowned in a bath, or a sink. The water in his lungs was tap water."

"No..."

I nodded. "Yes, so you had better start talking, Costas. Because we are interrogating Yeltsin too, and here's the interesting thing about Yeltsin. They want him in Russia on several counts of murder, drug trafficking, extortion—you know the kind of thing. And Russian prisons are not quite as comfortable as ours, especially as Yeltsin has a few enemies back home he is not keen to run into. So in exchange for a lenient sentence here, I think Peter Yeltsin will be keen to be cooperative."

Costas' eyes had gone hollow, and he looked like he might throw up. "I had nothing to do with Am's murder. I am not a killer. I panicked when you refused to close the case, only because I was scared my wife and kids would get to know about my affair with Jose. It was a stupid thing to do, but I told him, just fire a couple of times over their heads, then get out of there!"

Dehan sighed like she was bored. "I'm hearing a lot of words there, Varoufakis, but I ain't hearing no content. You already told us all that. Now, let's start where Dr. Jose Robles tells you about the LightYear Corporation's offer."

He buried his face in his hands and I heard him mutter, "Oh, dear God..."

"What happened, Costas? Did Robles start turning on you? Did he threaten to tell your wife, your boss? Did he threaten to leak it to the press that you hung out at the Dare 2 Dream?"

"I don't hang out there! I went there once!"

"On whose suggestion?"

"His, of course!"

"And now he was turning that against you, threatening you with it, just for laughs."

He didn't answer. I said, "Is that what happened, Costas?"

"Yes, kind of."

Dehan pressed him again. "So when he told you about the LightYear Corporation's offer, you went to Am and told him that Robles was planning to take the offer and cut him out."

"No, that's not how it happened."

"You persuaded Agnes to go out for the night. Where did you send her? To Dr. Meigh's?"

"No."

"You called Robles and you and Am waited for him, and when he came in, you shot him."

"No . . ." He shook his head. "You're wrong."

"No?" She stood and leaned across the table, pointing her finger at him. "Come on, Costas! You know how this works! Do you *really* think you can get away with this? We have your admission on tape that you tried to scare us off the investigation! That means one thing and one thing only, goddamn it! *It means you're guilty!*"

Beads of sweat had broken out on his forehead, and I could see his hands were shaking. "I asked the deputy inspector to appoint a team who would dig deep because I wanted to find out who had killed Jose. I would not have done such a stupid thing if I had killed him myself . . ."

Dehan didn't let him finish: "Unless you had framed Agnes!"

"But Gutierrez already suspected her! Why would I . . ."

"And that's a question you are going to enjoy asking the jury! Right? Come on, Costas! You know we can do this all day! You conspired to assassinate two police officers to cover up your crime. You're a DA, for crying out loud! You know how this works! The sooner you come clean, the easier it goes!"

He drew breath to answer, but I asked him, "How did you meet Am?"

"What?"

"How did you meet Am, Costas?"

"I . . . At Jose's house. He was leaving one day as I was arriving."

"Were they lovers?"

"I . . . I don't know. Possibly."

"Were you interested in Am? Sexually?"

He hesitated, frowned, then shook his head. "No! You're confusing me. No. I mean, he was good-looking, but . . ."

"You stayed in contact."

"Not really . . ."

"This is easy for us to check, Costas. Besides . . ." I gave a small laugh. "You either stayed in touch or you didn't. 'Not really' means you spoke again. When and why?"

"All right! I called him! Once!"

"What for?"

"To ask him out for a drink."

Dehan uttered an exclamation under her breath and looked away. I nodded and gave a look that suggested we were guys and a woman would never understand the way we operate. "Okay, let's take this easy. One step at a time." He began to relax. "So, when Jose came to you for legal advice about LightYear's offer, what did you advise him?"

"I told him it was very dangerous. The offer was huge, he would have become a very rich man, but he would have been in breach of contract as well as guilty of various criminal offenses."

Dehan interrupted. "Just let me ask you something. You say you don't know if Am and Jose were lovers. When you saw Am leaving Jose's house, what the hell did you think they had been doing? Playing cards?"

Costas bridled. "I imagined they had been discussing work. They *were* collaborating, remember!"

I grunted. "So you did know that they were collaborating."

He swallowed. "Yes . . ."

"So when Jose told you about the LightYear offer, did you think of telling Am?"

He saw the trap when it was too late. He was already in it and there was no way out. He closed his eyes. "Yes, but it is not the way you're making it seem."

Dehan exploded. "Oh, *really*? How are we making it seem, Costas? That you can't keep it in your pants, and you wouldn't know a faithful relationship if it bit you on the ass? Is that how we make it seem? Tell this reactionary, Republican bitch something. While you're offering your liberal ass to all takers around town, what is your wife doing back home? Is she washing up, cleaning your house, feeding your kids?"

"I am not the monster you are making me out to be!"

I sounded the voice of reason. "Let's get back on task. Did you warn Am that Jose might cut him out?"

"Yes."

Dehan snarled, "Betrayal comes really easy to you, doesn't it, Costas?"

"It wasn't betrayal! He had been treating me like shit!"

Again he saw it too late. Clamped his mouth shut and screwed up his eyes. I gave him a moment to realize he was sunk. Then I asked, "In what way was he treating you like shit?"

He didn't open his eyes, just shook his head. "He was being the way he was sometimes."

"Can you be a little more precise?"

He opened his eyes and sagged. "He was taunting me. He had this thing: he was attracted to people who were more powerful than him. He would start a new relationship by being very submissive, giving himself completely, until he found a weakness in the other person, and then he would start to attack that weakness, until he had that person completely enslaved. It was compulsive, and he would move from one relationship to another, leaving a trail of broken people in his wake. My weakness, he soon discovered, was my wife and children." He looked at Dehan. "Whatever you may think, I love them, and I would never do anything to hurt them. I had never been with a man until . . ." He gave a bitter laugh. "Until Jose discovered my latent weakness. I was fascinated by him."

Dehan's voice was quieter now. "So when he started to change . . ."

"I resented him. I saw that he was drawing Am in, and that he planned to steal his research and his ideas, so I arranged to meet him, to warn him."

I frowned. "So, I am not clear, did you and Am Nielsen become lovers?"

"No! I am not gay! It was just Jose! It was something weird that happened to me with him! I can't explain it!"

I smiled, not unkindly, guy to guy again. "And when he started threatening your wife and kids, that soon cured you of whatever it was."

"You can say that again!"

I raised an eyebrow at him. "I had a similar experience last night."

"Look, I . . ."

"Having your wife threatened will focus your mind. It strikes at our most primal instincts. I understand how you must have felt."

"I'd do anything for my family. But, Stone, I did not plan to hurt you or Carmen. I consider you friends. I just needed you to back off."

"I understand. I figure most people would have done something similar."

"My wife, my kids . . ."

"So when Jose threatened that, you arranged with Am to kill him and frame Agnes."

He stared at me wide-eyed. "*No!*"

"Give me a single reason why I should believe you."

He licked his lips. He looked at Dehan but found no sympathy there, then looked back at me. "Come on, Stone! You have to believe me! I could not murder anybody! And not Agnes! Jesus! I was really fond of Agnes! I would never hurt her!"

I raised an eyebrow, and Dehan gave a short, dry laugh. She said, "You were fond of Agnes?"

"Of course I was! She was a beautiful person! Jesus! She was quiet and shy, but she was also very smart and kind and gentle. She was the only person *he* respected."

I leaned forward. "*What?*"

"He adored her."

I shook my head. "How do you know this?"

He looked very confused. "We hung out together. Me and Agnes were close . . ."

There was a knock on the door. Gomez poked her head in. "You got a moment, Detective?"

I stood and stepped out. The door closed behind me. "We got Yeltsin, sir. He's being processed downstairs. His partner, Boris, is in the hospital. Seems you got him."

SEVENTEEN

I stepped back into the interrogation room and leaned against the wall by the door. Dehan restarted the recording and said, "Detective Stone has reentered the room."

Costas stared at me, and I held his eye. "They just brought Yeltsin in. He's being processed downstairs."

He dropped his eyes and stared at his hands on the table in front of him. "I swear I did not hire him to kill you, Stone. I would never do that."

"Be smart, Costas. You know what this means. When we start talking to him, he is going to sell you down the river. When the jury hear his testimony, and then hear from your own mouth that you hired him . . ." I shook my head. "You need to get real. Start telling the truth."

"For God's sake, Stone. I *am* telling you the truth."

I sighed noisily and sat. Dehan said, "You want us to believe that Agnes, who was desperately in love with Robles, was also your close pal; that you had some kind of ménage à trois going on, in which she never got to sleep with lover boy, but you did, and she was down with that?"

He screwed up his face. "*What?*" Then he laughed. "She was just his beard! She had no interest in him that way! They were friends! She was probably the only real friend he had, because he couldn't get to her."

I suppressed a smile. Dehan leaned across the table, frowning, curious. "Are you telling me that Robles and Shine were just friends?"

"Yes! That was the whole point of 'Jose and Agnes'! Anyone who was close to them knew that. He saw her as . . ." He shrugged, searching for the word. "I suppose almost like a mother figure. She was so *tolerant*! My God! He would say and do the most outrageous things, and she would just kind of smile, this long-suffering smile, and make some dry, witty comment to me, and we would laugh. I adore her. She was the sweetest, kindest woman you could imagine. But she was so painfully shy, few people ever got to know her as she really was."

"Was?"

He groaned and sighed. "Come on, Carmen! You know that's bullshit! It's called reported speech! You're telling a story, you put it in the past tense. I haven't heard from her in a couple of weeks!"

I said, "Where did you send her?"

"I don't know what you're talking about."

"You and Am decided to kill Robles. With the same elastic morality you displayed toward your wife and family, you decided to frame her and make her disappear. He had access to the weapons, you had access to the people who could give her a new identity."

"That is *absurd*! Can you hear yourself? She has a career, for Christ's sake! A house! A life! Friends!"

There was a knock on the door, and Gomez put her head in again.

"You asked me to let you know when the suspect was in the interrogation room. He has been formally charged."

I grunted, thanked her, and stood. "You are not doing yourself any favors, Costas. If you were the DA in this case, what would you be thinking right now?" I turned to Dehan. "Come on, let's let Mr. Varoufakis think for a while. We'll go and have a chat with Mr. Yeltsin."

At the door, I stopped and looked back at him. "How did you meet Yeltsin, Costas? He hasn't been prosecuted in New York."

"I wouldn't be stupid enough to use someone I had prosecuted, Stone. He was a friend of Am's, from the shooting range."

I smiled. "Better and better."

We took a walk to the coffee machine and got two paper cups of nasty black liquid. She leaned against the wall, and we stared at each other for a bit. Finally she shook her head.

"Whichever way I look at it, it's bullshit, Stone."

"I think what he said about Agnes is true. It makes sense of a lot of things we didn't understand. It is also very interesting."

She shrugged. "It doesn't change anything."

I nodded a few times. "Maybe. Whatever Yeltsin tells us will be key."

We went in. His wrists had been manacled to the table. He was six foot but strongly built, lean, and muscular. His face was alert and his expression predatory. He didn't look worried, just slightly mad. His right hand was bandaged, and two of the fingers were in splints.

We sat. I said, "You've been read your rights. Do you want an attorney present, or are you willing to talk to us?"

"I want deal. You give me deal, I don't need lawyer. You don't give me deal, you can fuck off."

"What kind of deal?"

"I tell you everything. I give you DA. I walk."

I laughed, not a lot, but enough to let him know I thought he was ridiculous. "You tried to assassinate me and my wife last night. You think I'm going to let you walk?"

He nodded. "Yuh."

"Not going to happen, Peter. You're wanted in California, Arizona, and Texas, and here you are charged with conspiracy to murder two officers of the law. You are doing time. We can talk about how much time, but you are doing time."

He muttered something in Russian. His eyes were very pale and looked amused. "He tell me not hurt you. He say, 'Oh! You are good people! Friend! No hurt them. Just scare a little.'" He sneered and said something that sounded like, "*Mudack!* There is no conspiracy to kill police officers. Only scare. But I have other information. More interesting. About pussy boy Am. You want to know, we talk deal."

"Yeah? You'd better give me more than that, Yeltsin. Right now I can nail you both just on forensic evidence."

He grunted a laugh. "You can nail shit. My lawyer make you look like asshole in court. Your DA kills pussy boy Am. I can prove, conclusive, and more. He is fucking killer. Not just pussy boy, also professor at university, Dr. Robles, and other professor, Dr. Shine. He kill all of them. I can prove conclusive, but I need deal. No deal, no proof."

Dehan leaned forward. "You are telling us that Assistant District Attorney Costas Varoufakis murdered Dr. Jose Robles, Dr. Agnes Shine, and Dr. Robles' student, Americano Nielsen?"

"That is what I just tell you, *sooka*. I tell you nothing more until I have deal from DA."

I sighed noisily, leaned back in my chair, and laughed quietly. "I hear a lot of talk." I looked up and held his eye. "I hear a lot of talk from a sissy who got his ass kicked last night by my *wife*." I looked at Dehan and we both laughed. "But words are cheap. Especially the ones I am hearing right now. Anyone can make accusations, Yeltsin. Let me see some substance. Like I told you, on forensic evidence alone, you and Varoufakis are going down. If you have something earth shattering, let's have a glimpse. Let me see some of it."

He wasn't drawn by the taunts. He glanced at Dehan a moment, then turned back to me. "I tell you where and how the DA drowns Am. I tell you why. I tell you how he is put him in the river. I tell you how he is kill Dr. Shine so no leave no sign off blood. I tell you where body is put in water. I tell you how he organize Dr. Robles' death and I tell you why. I tell you everything you are need know, every detail. If I no give you every detail of all three murder, no deal for me. You can write it like that. I sign. But deal is, no charge. I tell you, I go free."

I rubbed my chin and looked at Dehan. She gave a small nod. I said, "We need to discuss this with the DA."

We left him in the room and made our way to the deputy inspector's office. I knocked, and he barked, "Come!"

When we pushed in, the DA was there with him. The inspector stood. "John, Carmen, you know Denise Davis, the district attorney . . ."

We shook and muttered greetings, which I cut short and said, "I'm going to cut right to the chase. Yeltsin is offering us Varoufakis on a plate. He says he can prove that Varoufakis killed Dr. Robles, Dr. Shine, and Am Nielsen. He claims he can tell us where Dr. Shine's body was dumped in the river, and he can prove it all."

The DA frowned. "Do you believe him?"

I gave half a shrug. "In a sense, that's irrelevant, ma'am. He's willing to accept a deal that specifies that if he cannot provide satisfactory proof, there is no deal."

The inspector pointed at a couple of chairs. "Sit down, Detectives. Let's take this a step at a time. First of all, in a nutshell, what *is* the theory right now? Because I confess this case has me *confused*!"

I gestured at Dehan. "Detective Dehan proposed the current theory, and it seems Yeltsin may be about to confirm it. Perhaps she had better outline it."

"Sir, ma'am, this case is all about Dr. Jose Robles' compulsive need for dominant, sadomasochistic relationships."

Davis' eyebrows shot up and she said, "Oh!"

The inspector sat back in his chair and said, "Indeed . . . ?"

Dehan ignored them and plowed on. "Since he has been at the university, he has engaged in several of these relationships, which he starts in the passive role of a masochist, and then, having identified his partner's weakness, he switches so that he becomes the dominant sadist.

"It is key to the case that he did not have this kind of relationship with Dr. Shine, though they both allowed everybody to believe they had.

"Recently, ADA Varoufakis met Dr. Robles, and they became lovers. Initially, the ADA was the dominant partner, but pretty soon Robles realized that Varoufakis was devoted to his wife and children. This was his weakness, and Robles exploited it, threatening to reveal their relationship to the media and destroy his family. Right there is his motive for killing Robles.

"Now, meantime, Robles had another lover, a student and research assistant by the name of Americano Nielsen. Am was very brilliant, particularly in Robles' own field of lithium-ion-generated electricity. They worked closely together on research to develop a battery, and a motor, that could basically make petrol obsolete. Obviously this research—or at least as much of it as was conducted by Robles—belonged to the university. But, unbeknown to them, the LightYear Corporation approached Robles and made him an offer to let them have the research, and they would make him very rich.

"And that right there is where Varoufakis saw his means. He told Am about the offer and told him that Robles planned to cut him out. Between them, they plotted to kill him and frame Agnes, whom they also killed and dumped in one of the rivers somewhere.

"When Costas saw that we were going to unearth his relationship with Robles, he killed Am and faked his confession. When Stone didn't buy the confession, he panicked and hired Yeltsin to, so he says, scare us. I think that's probably true. It may be that Yeltsin was the hit man who killed Am. We'll have to wait and see."

She stopped talking, and they were both quiet for a while. Then the inspector nodded and cleared his throat. "Very clear and succinct, Carmen, thank you. John, your opinion?"

"So far, the only concrete evidence we have is a few statements and the forensic evidence showing that Yeltsin shot at us and that Robles and Agnes did not drink from their glasses of wine. Practically nothing. The case as Detective Dehan has set it out hinges on Yeltsin's testimony, or Varoufakis' confession. He, incidentally, admits trying to scare us but denies vehemently that he was involved in the murders." I turned to the DA. "The bottom line is, ma'am, whether you are prepared to offer him immunity from prosecution."

She looked at Dehan. "What's your advice, Detective Dehan?"

"On balance, I think it's worth it. If his testimony is as probative as he says, we need Varoufakis put away for the rest of his life. If it's a crock, we'll find out, and Yeltsin goes down. We may be able to take Varoufakis down too, but on lesser charges."

Davis turned to me. "Stone?"

"My advice would be to offer him the deal, but make it watertight."

She sighed and nodded. "It's hard to believe. Costas was a good man. Just shows, you never really know anybody, do you? I'll call the office and have them draft the document."

She stood and left the room. I stood and looked at the inspector. "We'll go and give the boys the good news."

Outside, as I closed the door, I said, "Let's go and see Costas first."

He looked up as we came in. His eyes and nose were swollen, like he'd been crying. Dehan stayed by the door, and I sat opposite him.

"I've just spoken to the DA. She's just agreed to a deal with Yeltsin. He's going to provide testimony that proves you killed Robles, Agnes, and Am. In exchange, he gets immunity from prosecution. Is there anything you want to tell me, Costas?"

His eyes were wide. He leaned forward, shaking his head. "This is insane! He *can't*! He *can't* do that because *I didn't kill them*! For crying out loud, John! *I wanted this case investigated!* I panicked when I thought you were going to expose my relationship with Jose! I did something very stupid in trying to scare you! I own to that! But you can't put me away for the rest of my life for murders I didn't commit!"

"You won't confess?"

"*No!*"

"Then get a lawyer, Costas. A good one."

I called the sergeant and told her to take him down to the cells and let him call his attorney. After that, Dehan and I went back to the coffee machine and got more dirty black water and stood in silence, not drinking. After five minutes, Denise Davis appeared with a folder. She handed it to me and stared into my eyes. "Here goes nothing."

I nodded.

Yeltsin was sitting, looking smug. He raised an eyebrow as Dehan closed the door and we moved to the table. "You got a deal for me?"

Dehan sat and started recording. When she'd finished the preliminaries, I showed him the folder. "This is the deal, Peter, on exactly the terms you proposed, as stated on the previous recording. You give us proof of Costas Varoufakis' guilt in the murders of Jose Robles, Agnes Shine, and Americano Nielsen, and you get immunity from prosecution."

"Yeah," he said, and leered at Dehan. "I tell you whole story. Give me, I sign."

I pulled out the document and slid it across the desk to him. It was short and concise. He read through it carefully, pursed his lips, and nodded. He held out his manacled hand without looking up. "Give me pen, I sign."

I handed him my pen. "Now, start talking."

EIGHTEEN

He held his manacled wrists toward me. "You no gonna prosecute me. You can undo this, no?"

I showed him an expressionless face. "Talk. Let's see what you've got. Right now, you're the punk who tried to shoot my wife last night. Show me I'm wrong and I'll take the cuffs off."

He slouched back.

"Okay, couple of month ago, I start shooting at Coyne Park, in Yonkers. Is ten, fifteen minutes' drive. I know guns. I like guns. But I am only professional there. Everybody else is bigmouth, no experience. Then I meet Am." He laughed. "Americano! He's nice guy, always joking, making funny. But he knows guns. He never been in army, but he know guns. He have the mind and the heart of a warrior. Cold inside. I know. I recognize. I tell him, you wasting your fucking time in university. I introduce you to people, you can make big money doing what you love." He shrugged his big shoulders. "But he don't want to know. 'No,' he say me, 'No, I gonna make an electric motor!'" He threw his head back and burst out laughing. "He is going to make electric motor! Electric motor is going to make him rich man, like Elon Musk!"

Dehan said, "What made him think that?"

"Because his professor is telling him, 'You and me going to

make electric motor, with fantastic battery, fastest car in world.' He tell me, 'Peter, this car going to go two hundred mile an hour, minimum! Accelerate zero to one hundred in one second.' It's going to be fucking spaceship.

"Okay, so then week is passing, two weeks, and he ask me, 'Hey, Peter, you in the Russian Army?' I tell him yeah, I was in special unit. We do a lot of bad things. He tell me, 'My friend is looking for tough guy like you to help make a job.' I tell him, I am not cheap. He wants me to kill somebody, it is going to cost ten thousand dollars minimum. If is university professor, it is going to be more."

I said, "Names."

"Not yet. So he tell me this is very expensive. I say to him, 'Look, you can do this. You don't need spend money on professional like me. I only advise you, tell you how, two thousand bucks, you make the job. He think about it and he says okay.

"So this the job: professor who was going to make super car with him, Dr. Jose Robles. Now he is going to sell idea to big company." He thought for a moment. "There were two company, LightYear was one, then Electron was other. He was interested in LightYear. But he not tell Am about this. Am is find out because . . ." He screwed up his face. "Dr. Robles' lawyer is tell Am about it! So I am saying, what the fuck? What the fuck, man? You bring lawyer, he sit down here with me, and you both going to tell me fucking everything. His *lawyer* is telling *you*? Somebody trying to screw somebody, right?

"Okay, so then lawyer is Costas Varoufakis. And it don't take me long find out that lawyer Varoufakis is fucking Robles, and Robles is threatening to sell story to TV. So Varoufakis and Am making a plan to fuck Robles." He threw back his head and laughed out loud again. "Everybody fucking somebody."

I said, "So you advised them?"

"Yeah, they come to my house. We drink, we make plan. They tell me everything. I tell them, okay, this how you going to do it. You kill him and you kill woman. She going to be easy to kill.

Then, he like wine, so you make it look like they been having drink, she is in love with him, everybody in love with Dr. Robles, she jealous, she kill him. Some fingerprints on gun, on glasses. You take her, put rocks in her clothes, and put her in river. She is probably in Bahamas by now. She killed him and she run away. Simple."

I shrugged. "It's a story. Where's the proof?"

He looked at me with dead eyes. "I not finished yet. Give me pen and paper."

I handed him my pen again and a slip of paper. He scrawled down a series of numbers alongside dates and an address downtown.

"Four payments of five hundred dollars in cash. Nielsen goes with Varoufakis to this ATM to collect money. You check Varoufakis account, you see he makes these withdrawals. This money is to pay me for my advice on the murder of Robles and Shine."

I glanced at Dehan. She took the piece of paper and left the room. Yeltsin said, "More. I was at house when they prepare for killing. I see Am kill Agnes. He use his arm in armlock and strangle her. Varoufakis run upstairs and sick in toilet. Am is cool, he set glasses out on tables by chairs, pour wine, only a little in each glass, pour half the bottle down sink, then Varoufakis come down. I go check all his sick is gone. I come down and Am call Robles on Agnes house telephone. He tell him to come over to Agnes house. He has to argue, but finally Robles is agree. So if you looking for fingerprints on Agnes house phone, you going to find Am's prints. They are going to be last prints on telephone."

I took my cell from my pocket and called Joe.

"John, how's it going?"

"Joe, can you get a team over to Dr. Agnes Shine's house, dust her telephone, the landline, see if Am Nielsen's prints are on it? Theory is he was the last person to use it."

"Sure. I'll get a team over there right away."

"Thanks." I hung up. Yeltsin continued:

"Dr. Robles arrive. Am let him in, close door, and pull gun.

'You go and you sit down. Pick up fucking glass. Put down.' Bang! Eight times. Bang! Bang! Bang! Then wipe gun and put it in Agnes hand. Take Agnes to river with her ID documents. Finish."

"Where, exactly?"

"Through park at back of house. Is easy, into Pugsley Creek." He made a face and carried on. "So, everything going nicely. We leave it like this and soon case is closed. But Varoufakis want to be clever. You can be too clever. Varoufakis too fucking clever. He want to make sure everybody believing he is innocent man. So he call your chief, 'Hey, I want you put your best men on this case.' But his best man is good cop, fucking pit bull, never let go, huh? He can smell something wrong, something wrong. So Varoufakis say me, 'We going to tie up loose ends.' He write a confession for Am. We take to Am and I put gun to Am's head."

"Your friend."

"I have two friends, Detective: me and money. I put gun to Am's head: write fucking confession on your phone. He write. I take him to toilet, I fill sink with water, and I put in his head until he dead. Then we take to the river and throw in. You going to find fingerprints on arm are from my hand. Now, I going to ask you, what motive I have for killing Am Nielsen? No motive. Now I asking you, what motive Varoufakis has? Good fucking motive. Same man who employ me to scare you.

"Last thing I give you. In my apartment, where your police find me, there you find burner telephone, Samsung, on table. This Samsung is one I use for communicate with Varoufakis. You going to find on it the calls he is make to me, before I make him use burner. Then you going to find the number of his burner. Maybe you get lucky and find that phone in his house. So, you got the money, you got Am's prints, you got my prints, you got the telephone, and you got my testimony. You got proof."

"What about the research? What happened to that?"

He stared at me a long time. There was something odd in his eyes. I couldn't make out if it was humor or insolence; maybe both. He shrugged. "I don't know what happen to that. Maybe is still at university. Maybe LightYear get it. Maybe Electron."

The door opened, and Dehan came in. I stood. "Okay, Peter. We'll see if this all checks out. If it does, it looks like you've got your deal."

I stepped out and had the uniform take Yeltsin down to his cell while the tapes of the interview were taken to the inspector and the DA. Then I called Joe again.

"Stone, you again so soon? People will start to talk."

I forced a laugh. "One last thing, Joe. The prints on Am's arm. Yeltsin—the guy who shot at us last night—he says those prints will be his. Can you check that?"

"Sure thing, I'll be in touch."

"Thanks."

Dehan put her hand on my shoulder. "Newman has requested his financials. We got him, Stone."

I nodded. "Yeah. We got him . . ."

"You okay?" I nodded again. She shrugged. "Agnes is dead. You were sure she was still alive. I'm sorry."

I smiled. "It was so hard to get a handle on any of their personalities. Hers more than most. Sounds like she was a nice person."

"Academics. They're all crazy, right? What you see is definitely not what you get."

"For sure."

The inspector put his head out his door. "Stone, Dehan, we got confirmation. They're sending his records over, but they were able to confirm the withdrawals. We have him. It is a very sad day in many ways, but well done to both of you. A superb piece of work. Well done. I'll let you know as soon as we get confirmation on the prints and the rest of it. How's the shoulder, John?"

"Nothing a Bushmills won't fix, sir. Yeltsin tells me Agnes' body was dumped in Pugsley Creek, at the back of her house. It has probably been dragged out into the East River by now, but we should conduct a search anyway."

"Yes, indeed. I'll see to it." He nodded, then smiled. "Bushmills, excellent choice! Well, I'll see you Monday, then!"

"I think we'll go and give Dr. Meigh the news, sir. I believe La Piccola Liguria in Port Washington does rather good oysters and a sirloin steak in black pepper and brandy sauce that is really something special."

He looked vaguely surprised. "Oh, well, that is very thoughtful of you, John. Thank you, and you two have a lovely evening."

"Thank you, sir. We will do our best. After that, we're going to Goa, for Christmas. I owe it to Dehan as part of a bet."

He laughed. "Gotta go ta Goa!"

"Never gets old, sir."

We went down the stairs, collected our coats, and stepped out into the icy wind. It was only midday, but the heavy, bellying clouds and the dull, uniform gray light made it feel like early evening.

We made it to the car and climbed in before Dehan said, "Okay, what's going on? What did I miss, get wrong, overlook, or fail to take into account?"

I smiled, started the engine, and reversed out of the lot. "That is not very nice, Dehan. I take you out for a romantic evening and you impute all kinds of dishonest motives to me."

"Yadda yadda..."

"Seriously, Dehan. I just want to wrap the case up, inform Dr. Meigh, and take you to dinner. It *is* almost Christmas!"

She raised an eyebrow, and we set off toward Throggs Neck and Long Island.

―――

DR. MEIGH OPENED THE DOOR, and the slight widening of her eyes said she was startled.

"Detectives... We are just having lunch..."

"And we are on our way to lunch, but we thought we'd just drop in to let you know that the case has been closed."

"Oh, well, that's very good of you. Thank you." She hesitated, unsure whether to close the door.

I waited, smiling, until it became awkward and then added, "You must be curious to know who did it. I'm afraid I also have some rather sad news for you."

She sighed and her shoulders slumped. "You had better come in."

"We won't keep you long, Dr. Meigh. It shouldn't take more than a couple of minutes."

She forced a smile. "Of course. It is thoughtful of you to come all this way." She led us into the drawing room, where a fire was burning in the grate, reflecting off the baubles and tinsel on a vast Christmas tree and throwing ghostly reflections against the windowpanes. She sat, perched on the edge of a calico armchair. Dehan took the sofa, and I took the other chair.

I said, "Perhaps your husband would like to join us."

Dehan glanced at me and frowned. Meigh said, "No, that is quite unnecessary, Detective. What is the news you have for me?"

I spread my hands. "Cutting a long story short, Dr. Meigh, Peter Yeltsin has confessed that he was employed by Assistant District Attorney Costas Varoufakis to kill Dr. Robles."

"Really? How extraordinary."

"Yes, Robles and Varoufakis were having an affair, and Robles was threatening to tell the media. One of his power games. Varoufakis panicked and employed Yeltsin to kill him. Part of the plan was to frame Agnes, kill her, and dump her body in the river, to make it look as though she had killed him and fled."

"Oh." The only sign of emotion was that her face went very rigid.

I waited a moment, then said, "I imagine you'll miss her."

"Of course, we all will."

"Of course, Am was also a part of the plot. There were three of them, Costas, Yeltsin, and Am."

"I see."

"Am's motive was that the LightYear Corporation had made Robles an offer to buy his research, and Robles admitted to Costas that he was going to make the sale and cut Am out. So Costas and Am teamed up."

"Well, thank you for taking the time to bring me the news..."

Dehan made to stand. I said, "There is just one thing."

Meigh sighed. "Yes, Detective Stone."

"There was a second corporation who apparently also made an offer for Robles' and Am's research. The Electron Corporation. I don't know what happened to that offer. The one Robles apparently went for was the LightYear offer."

"I see. Anything else?"

"I just wondered if you had been approached by Electron...?"

"No, of course not."

"Okay, well, we'll leave you to your lunch. You'll be off to Maine soon, I imagine."

"Yes, tomorrow in fact, if we can get away."

She labored the last words as she stood. We followed her to the hall, and she led the way across the hall toward the front door. As she reached it, I snapped my fingers and gave a small laugh. "My gloves!"

I turned on my heel and marched back. I heard her voice behind me, "Detective!"

As I reached the dining room, I grabbed the handle and pushed open the door. I could hear Meigh's feet running behind me.

He was sitting with his back to me, eating what appeared to be a chocolate mousse. I glanced at Meigh, and the distress on her face told me I was right. Behind her, moving as though in slow motion, was Dehan, both running toward me. I looked back into the room and said, "Hello, Agnes."

Her hair was cut short and dyed very black. The clothes were a man's clothes, jacket, shirt, and tie, but the face was easily recognizable as Agnes Shine's. She stood and turned to face me.

Dr. Meigh grabbed my arm in both her hands and pulled at me. Her face was twisted with all the emotion she had failed to show before. "You are not allowed in here!"

I spoke quietly, "It's over, Dr. Meigh. You very nearly got away with it. But the game is up."

"*No!*"

Agnes came around her chair and took Meigh in her arms. Meigh seemed to collapse, sobbing into her neck.

I turned to Dehan, whose mouth was slightly open. "You better call for a patrol car, and the crime scene team." Then I turned to Agnes and Meigh. "Dr. Patricia Meigh, Dr. Agnes Shine, I am placing you both under arrest for the murders of Dr. Jose Robles and Americano Nielsen, and for the theft of intellectual property from University College New York."

EPILOGUE

The weather outside was frightful, but the fire, where it was crackling in the hearth, was quite delightful. Big, fat flakes were falling past the window, shrouding everything in a blanket of frozen white, while a warm, wavering amber glow filled the room and glinted off the large red, orange, and yellow balls on the tree.

I sat on the sofa with my feet on Dehan's lap and sipped a large glass of mulled wine, watching her face while she gazed at the flames.

"That has to have been the most confusing case we have ever had."

I made a "hmmm" noise and nodded.

"How did you know that Agnes was there?"

I shrugged. "It was the simplest explanation. It all fell into place when Yeltsin mentioned the Electron Corporation. I'd had my doubts about Meigh from the start. She had shown no emotion whatsoever about Agnes' disappearance. At first that seemed normal because we didn't think they were very close. But then when it emerged that they were actually very close friends, her indifference made no sense at all, unless she knew Agnes was safe."

She nodded. "Yeah, when you put it like that."

"That was when I asked you to look into the births, deaths, marriages, et cetera relating to Meigh. You found out that she wasn't married, and that she owned a house in Maine, where they were going for Christmas."

"That's why it surprised me when you asked if her husband wanted to join us. You knew she wasn't married."

"But that day we were checking on Robles' research, I had seen her with a man, and they were behaving like a couple. I assumed at the time it was her husband. But then it began to dawn on me. Maybe it wasn't her husband, but her lover. So while you were doing a background search on Meigh, I did a background search on Agnes and found out that she really was a brilliant economist, and was on the boards of a number of corporations. When Yeltsin mentioned Electron, I recognized it as one of the corporations she was connected with."

She snorted. "Son of a gun. So when Meigh realized the potential for the research Robles and Am were conducting, she suggested to Agnes that they should sell it to Electron."

"Yup. Meigh knew that the real brains behind the research was Am, so she recruited him, and soon discovered he was able and willing to do more than just design batteries. And when LightYear came along and complicated matters by making Robles an offer, and Robles seemed determined to accept it and cut Am out, they decided he had to die."

"So it was Am who killed Robles."

"Oh yes, that was clear from the beginning. And note that neither Am nor Meigh had any interest in wine."

"Okay," she said, turning from the fire to look at me. "But how does Yeltsin fit into all this? We had it all sewn up!"

"Meigh had it all sewn up. Did you notice the security company that the university uses?"

"No."

"VMS, stands for Veteran Military Security. A lot of major corporations who have very sensitive, valuable material use them, because they only employ very high-caliber military vets. But like many high-level security companies, these guys don't only supply security guards, they provide the whole range of personnel, all the way up to mercenaries. Meigh is a very clever, subtle woman. When she and Agnes had first come up with her plan, she had recruited Yeltsin. She didn't have to go very far to look for him. He was on VMS' books. She was aware that Am could become a problem at some point in the future, so she had Yeltsin befriend him and keep an eye on him. As it turned out, she was right to do so, because when Costas showed up, demanding a deeper investigation and talking to Am about how Robles was planning A, to reveal their relationship to the media and B, to take LightYear's offer, it was clear that not only did Robles have to die, but Am had to take the fall for it. Hence the suicide."

"So the whole thing was planned and orchestrated by Meigh and Agnes, so that they could sell Robles' and Am's research to Electron."

"A company in which Agnes had a stack of shares."

"So Costas was telling the truth?"

"Costas was a fool, but apart from lying to his wife and trying to scare us off the case, he was telling the truth."

"But hang on a second there, big guy, that is a hell of a coincidence, isn't it? That Costas should employ Yeltsin to scare us?"

"Not a coincidence at all. Remember, Yeltsin had got Am to introduce him to Costas. In Yeltsin's story, it was to commit murder; in reality it was so he could keep tabs on them both. It was Yeltsin who offered himself to scare us off. Remember Costas told us that?"

"So basically Meigh and Agnes employed Yeltsin to manage the murder and keep track of what their pawns were doing. That is scary."

"Very subtle and very intelligent women."

"And the guy who called, who threatened to kill me?"

"Meigh's final attempt to scare us into accepting Am's confession and dropping the investigation. What caused us so much confusion was that Meigh and Costas both wanted the same thing, and each made an attempt to persuade us to give it up. Hers was more subtle, his was more desperate."

"And she offered you the name of the LightYear Corporation to lead you away from Electron and into accepting Am's suicide story."

"Yup."

"That was one hell of a risk Yeltsin took, offering that deal."

"He was never supposed to get caught. But when they realized it was inevitable, they came up with the idea of the deal. I imagine he was paid very well for that."

"And the four withdrawals of five hundred bucks each at the ATM, from Costas' account?"

"Simple, Am clones Costas' card. All too easy these days."

I sipped my wine and watched the flames for a while as it grew dark outside. "One thing I don't get, and will probably never get, is why Yeltsin gave us the name Electron."

"A slip of the tongue?"

"Maybe. You want your Christmas present now, or in the morning?"

"That depends, will I have to pack?"

"Yes."

"Then you'd better give it to me now . . ."

Don't miss JACK IN THE BOX. The riveting sequel in the Dead Cold Mystery series.

Scan the QR code below to purchase JACK IN THE BOX.

Or go to: righthouse.com/jack-in-the-box

NOTE: flip to the very end to read an exclusive sneak peak...

DON'T MISS ANYTHING!

If you want to stay up to date on all new releases in this series, with this author, or with any of our new deals, you can do so by joining our newsletters below.

In addition, you will immediately gain access to our entire *Right House VIP Library*, which includes many riveting Mystery and Thriller novels for your enjoyment!

righthouse.com/email

(Easy to unsubscribe. No spam. Ever.)

ALSO BY BLAKE BANNER

Up to date books can be found at:
www.righthouse.com/blake-banner

ROGUE THRILLERS
Gates of Hell (Book 1)
Hell's Fury (Book 2)

ALEX MASON THRILLERS
Odin (Book 1)
Ice Cold Spy (Book 2)
Mason's Law (Book 3)
Assets and Liabilities (Book 4)
Russian Roulette (Book 5)
Executive Order (Book 6)
Dead Man Talking (Book 7)
All The King's Men (Book 8)
Flashpoint (Book 9)
Brotherhood of the Goat (Book 10)
Dead Hot (Book 11)
Blood on Megiddo (Book 12)
Son of Hell (Book 13)

HARRY BAUER THRILLER SERIES
Dead of Night (Book 1)
Dying Breath (Book 2)
The Einstaat Brief (Book 3)
Quantum Kill (Book 4)
Immortal Hate (Book 5)
The Silent Blade (Book 6)
LA: Wild Justice (Book 7)

Breath of Hell (Book 8)
Invisible Evil (Book 9)
The Shadow of Ukupacha (Book 10)
Sweet Razor Cut (Book 11)
Blood of the Innocent (Book 12)
Blood on Balthazar (Book 13)
Simple Kill (Book 14)
Riding The Devil (Book 15)
The Unavenged (Book 16)
The Devil's Vengeance (Book 17)
Bloody Retribution (Book 18)
Rogue Kill (Book 19)
Blood for Blood (Book 20)

DEAD COLD MYSTERY SERIES
An Ace and a Pair (Book 1)
Two Bare Arms (Book 2)
Garden of the Damned (Book 3)
Let Us Prey (Book 4)
The Sins of the Father (Book 5)
Strange and Sinister Path (Book 6)
The Heart to Kill (Book 7)
Unnatural Murder (Book 8)
Fire from Heaven (Book 9)
To Kill Upon A Kiss (Book 10)
Murder Most Scottish (Book 11)
The Butcher of Whitechapel (Book 12)
Little Dead Riding Hood (Book 13)
Trick or Treat (Book 14)
Blood Into Wine (Book 15)
Jack In The Box (Book 16)
The Fall Moon (Book 17)
Blood In Babylon (Book 18)
Death In Dexter (Book 19)
Mustang Sally (Book 20)

A Christmas Killing (Book 21)
Mommy's Little Killer (Book 22)
Bleed Out (Book 23)
Dead and Buried (Book 24)
In Hot Blood (Book 25)
Fallen Angels (Book 26)
Knife Edge (Book 27)
Along Came A Spider (Book 28)
Cold Blood (Book 29)
Curtain Call (Book 30)

THE OMEGA SERIES
Dawn of the Hunter (Book 1)
Double Edged Blade (Book 2)
The Storm (Book 3)
The Hand of War (Book 4)
A Harvest of Blood (Book 5)
To Rule in Hell (Book 6)
Kill: One (Book 7)
Powder Burn (Book 8)
Kill: Two (Book 9)
Unleashed (Book 10)
The Omicron Kill (Book 11)
9mm Justice (Book 12)
Kill: Four (Book 13)
Death In Freedom (Book 14)
Endgame (Book 15)

ABOUT US

Right House is an independent publisher created by authors for readers. We specialize in Action, Thriller, Mystery, and Crime novels.

If you enjoyed this novel, then there is a good chance you will like what else we have to offer! Please stay up to date by using any of the links below.

Join our mailing lists to stay up to date -->
righthouse.com/email
Visit our website --> righthouse.com
Contact us --> contact@righthouse.com

 facebook.com/righthousebooks
 x.com/righthousebooks
 instagram.com/righthousebooks

EXCLUSIVE SNEAK PEAK OF...

JACK IN THE BOX

CHAPTER 1

It was spring, and all the trees that had been cold and naked during the long winter were now responding to the watery, early sun by sprouting small, succulent, bright green leaves. The air was chill, but I had the windows of my ancient Jaguar open, and Dehan, in her black leather jacket, was watching me through her aviators as the spring air whipped her black hair across her face. I glanced at her and smiled. She was a nice thing to smile at.

She spoke, outlining the facts.

"Thursday, October seventh, 2014. Helena Magnusson, thirty-five, drives to Underhill Community Center in the Bronx to teach her creative writing evening class. When she gets there, at five thirty, a parcel arrives for her by special delivery. When she opens it, it contains her husband Jack's head."

"Huh! Jack in the box."

"Don't interrupt. Jack Connors, fifty-two, mega-successful founder and CEO of Connors Communication, an advertising company that claims it specializes in 'persuasion engineering,' apparently a branch of neurolinguistic programming."

"Thinking outside the box."

"Are you done?" I nodded. She went on. "The ME said that

his head had been severed with exceptional precision in a single cut. He believed a razor-sharp samurai sword might have been used, or something of that sort. Blood residue on the neck tissue suggested that the man had been lying down when he was decapitated. He also detected traces of ketamine in the blood, suggesting he may have been rendered unconscious before being killed."

"But his eyes were open."

"Yes. So if he was drugged, he woke up before he was killed. The face was tested for fingerprints but none showed up. The rest of the body was never found, despite an extensive search of parks and rivers. What's left of him is probably in the East River somewhere."

"Not habeas corpus, but habeas caput."

"Caput?"

"Head."

"You're on fire today, Stone. Pretty much the only person to benefit from his death was his wife, who inherited a controlling share in the business. Apparently she later sold some of those shares in a private deal to Seth Greenway, the current CEO, and became a sleeping partner. She also inherited a brownstone beside Morningside Park, a weekend house outside New Haven, and another apartment in Boston. She used to lecture there in English literature. Financial gain does not seem to be much of a motive in her case, however, as she was already a rich woman in her own right, being *the* Helena Magnusson."

"Best-selling novelist of dubious talent. You say 'pretty much' the only person to gain from his death. Talk me through that."

"One day, Stone, you will actually read a case file from cover to cover."

I arched an eyebrow at her. "The day you do, perhaps."

She ignored me. We had come to Morningside Avenue. I turned left, and after four blocks, I turned left again into West 122nd. I pulled in between a green ash and a hydrant, killed the engine, and turned to Dehan. She took a deep breath and said:

"The only other person to benefit from his death was Seth Greenway."

"The current CEO."

"But I don't really buy that, Stone. I mean, how sure could he have been that he would get to take over?" She shrugged. "The big problems in this case, as always in a cold case, were a lack of forensic evidence and witnesses, but the lack of apparent motive was also a major stumbling block. Everyone, friends and workmates, agreed that Helena and Jack were the ideal couple and very much in love with each other, and at work everyone said Jack was a great boss."

I stuck out my bottom lip and grunted. "It's a very striking way to kill somebody, isn't it—severing the head. You can't get much more final than that."

She nodded. "It sends a message, as does putting it in a box and sending it to the wife."

"Almost," I said, "as though *she* were the killer's real target, not the husband."

"That had struck me. But a target for what, exactly?"

"Okay, let's go and talk to her."

We climbed out and made our way down the leafy, Victorian street that, in the age of baseball caps, cargo shorts, and smartphones, had somehow managed to retain some of its old grandeur and elegance. Hers was the second of a row of understated, three-story brownstones. It had a stone stoop with a magnificent balustrade up to equally magnificent heavy brown doors under a vaguely Egyptian-looking portico. I rang the bell and waited while Dehan went up and down on her toes a few times, chewing her lip and scanning the facade.

"What do you reckon, three million?"

I glanced at the other houses down the street. "Three, three and a half."

The door opened to reveal a smiling woman in her early twenties. She was wearing what appeared to be a surgeon's coat and had very blond hair and very blue eyes. Her voice was fruity and fluty.

"Hello, you are detectives who are calling earlier?"

We showed her our badges and Dehan said, "Detectives Dehan and Stone, we are here for Mrs. Magnusson."

She did a funny little bob with her knees and said, "Yoh, she is expectink you. Please follow."

The entrance hall was unexpectedly large. The floor was an intricate mosaic of hexagonal black and white tiles, with a deep, oxblood Persian rug thrown over it any old how. Large walnut doors stood closed on our left. Beyond them a broad, carpeted staircase rose to the second floor. To the right, a passage disappeared toward what I assumed was the kitchen.

We followed the blond girl in the surgeon's coat up the stairs and along a landing carpeted in the same oxblood red to a second set of walnut doors at the front of the house. There she knocked and went in.

"Madam, the detectives are here."

She waited for an answer we did not hear, then bobbed and smiled at us. "Please come in, yoh."

We went in and she closed the doors behind us. We were in a large drawing room with a magnificent bay window overlooking the street below. The floors were hardwood, strewn with Persian rugs, and the furniture, which was eclectic, seemed not to include anything later than the 1930s. A soft leather sofa sat opposite an iron fireplace, flanked by heavy lamp tables, and on either side of the fire there was a Chesterfield armchair. The paintings on the walls looked like minor impressionists, but they were originals.

Helena was standing by the sofa with her hands clasped in front of her. Her eyes were pale blue, and a small crease between her brows was the only expression on her face. A small frown for a small worry. Her hair was not so much tied up in a bun as tied up out of the way. Her cardigan, the same blue as her eyes, was somehow more noticeable than her pearls. Her shoes, like her skirt, were sensible. She did something with her mouth that, had she ever given it life, might have become a smile.

"Detectives," she said, as though she were considering the word.

We showed her our badges and Dehan spoke. "Mrs. Magnusson, I am Detective Carmen Dehan, and this is my partner, Detective John Stone."

Before she could continue, Helena gave her head a small shake. "You said on the telephone you wanted to talk about Jack . . ."

There was the faintest hint of an accent: a softening of the *t*s and *d*s, a narrowing of the vowels. I wondered if she was Norwegian or Danish. She gestured at the chairs. "Please, do sit down. Have you found something?"

We sat, and she sat almost perched on the edge of the sofa, with her knees together and her ankles to one side, her hands folded on her lap. Dehan shook her head.

"I'm afraid not, Mrs. Magnusson. My partner heads up a cold-cases unit at the Forty-Third Precinct. We periodically review cases that stalled for one reason or another, and we are having a look at your husband's case. I know it's distressing, but we were hoping you could talk us through it."

She raised her eyebrows and gave a little sigh through her nose. "There is so little to tell. I was teaching at Underhill Community Center." She glanced at us, as though realizing suddenly the statement needed an explanation. "So many people, not just young, but mainly older people, in boroughs like the Bronx, never have the opportunity, you know, to express themselves artistically." Her eyes drifted. "Most have nothing to say of any value, but sometimes, you know . . ." She looked at me and smiled. "Not often, you meet somebody with talent. After the class, my publisher was organizing a party at the Chadwick and Holstein offices in Manhattan; we were launching the new book. 2014, let me see . . ." Again her eyes drifted away, as though she were looking at hidden images within the wall. "*The Many Colors of Snow*. My husband was going to pick me up to take me there, but he called, um, one o'clock, about, and said he must come later. He was always so busy at work. So, I took my car. I was always a little early to the class, to prepare, and the young man came to my class . . ."

"Young man?"

"From UPS, I think. He gives me the box, asks me to sign for it, and leaves. I was of course very curious to see what . . ."

She seemed to freeze. Her gaze shifted to the rug, and she blinked several times in rapid succession. It was the only sign that she was feeling any kind of emotion. After a moment, she swallowed and said, "You know, it is such a long time since I have spoken about it. You would think . . . But, in any case, I had not ordered anything, I was not expecting anything, so naturally I was curious. So I opened the box and inside was a cool box, like for a picnic. I took it out, more curious now, and I opened the cool box."

Again she stopped, looked away, and bit her lip. She gave her head a small shake. "He was on his back, as though he was lying down. I have seen him like this more times than I can count, in the morning and in the evening. And he was staring right at me. He looked serious, a little surprised. Very . . ." She frowned at Dehan and ran her fingertips softly over her own cheek. "Very pale, because he had no blood in him. Of course he could not see me. I am told that I screamed, but I don't remember. I remember, the next thing, that I was in a chair, there were a lot of people, and somebody was giving me water from one of those disgusting plastic glasses. I didn't drink it. I could not drink it from such a plastic glass."

She took a deep breath and looked back at Dehan. "The police came, a doctor came, and some paramedics. They wanted me to go to hospital, or at least go home. But that is not the way we do things."

I smiled. "We?"

She met my smile with one of her own that was a little distant.

"In my family. My father was a very strong man. He taught me that we see first to our duties, and we express our emotions later, in private."

"So you went to the book launch?"

She nodded. "Yes, of course."

Dehan scratched her head and left a few stray hairs standing slightly on end. "Mrs. Magnusson, when was the last time you actually saw your husband?"

"At breakfast. We are both early risers, well, he was an early riser, and we always breakfasted together at six. Then he went to work and I went to my office. I work, naturally, from home."

I asked, "And the next communication you had with him?"

"At one o'clock, when he called to say he could not collect me from the community center."

"That would be his lunchtime?"

She looked a little surprised. "I imagine so, Detective Stone. Is that important?"

"I don't know. What did you do after you received the phone call?"

"I had lunch with some friends who were visiting from Boston, some fellow lecturers." She sighed and closed her eyes for a second. "One of them was a friend. The others were friends of his. The details are in the original statement I gave the police at the time."

"Did you go directly?"

She didn't answer for a moment and seemed to be remembering. "Yes," she said at last. "They were already here. I told them Jack would not be coming to the launch and we went. Again, I did tell the police . . ."

Dehan nodded. "I'm sure the detective at the time asked you all of this, Mrs. Magnusson, but sometimes time and reflection can cast a new light on things. Is there anyone you can think of, however remote or unlikely it may seem, who could have had a grudge against your husband?"

She smiled. It was an odd smile that seemed to suggest that

Dehan's question was somehow absurd. Her gaze drifted and she pointed at my chair. "He used to sit there, smoking a cigar in the evening. He liked cognac, the Rémy Martin Fine Champagne, XO . . . extra old." She made a disparaging face and gave a small laugh. "I think it is a vulgar drink in a vulgar bottle, but he likes it . . . He liked it." She took a deep breath and the laughter faded from her face. "Of course, I have asked myself this many times. Who? Who would want to do this? But I cannot answer that question. So many people in his life I did not know. I knew nothing of his work. In his personal life I can tell you that he had no enemies—few friends, but no enemies. At work . . ." She gave a delicate shrug. "I do not know. You would better ask Seth, and his colleagues."

Dehan nodded again. "Sure, we will do that." She hesitated a moment, then said, "Mrs. Magnusson, there is an outside possibility that you, and not your husband, were the focus of this attack. Had that crossed your mind?"

She blinked, and her eyebrows rose a fraction. "What on Earth can you mean?"

"My partner and I both agree that the fact that so much care was taken to send . . ."

She hesitated again, and Helena supplied the missing words: "My husband's head."

"Yes, the fact that so much trouble was taken to send it to you in that particular way suggests that you were, at least to some extent, a target in this crime."

"That had never occurred to me. It is obvious now that you say it, and I a crime writer . . ."

For a fleeting moment her bottom lip curled in, and she blinked away tears from her eyes. I said, "You were too close to it."

"No doubt."

"But you see that there was an attempt here to communicate something to you."

"Yes."

"This would suggest that the murderer knew you both, and considered himself..."

"Or herself."

"Yes, or herself, to have some kind of relationship with you. Seen from that perspective, does anyone come to mind? Can you think *what* they might have wanted to communicate?"

She shook her head, not in negation but as though daunted by the enormity of the task. "I shall have to think about it. I have not thought about this for a long time."

I nodded. "Of course. Mrs. Magnusson, I only have a couple more questions for you and then we'll leave you in peace. How did you get from the community center to the party on Madison Avenue, in Manhattan?"

She stared at me for a long moment.

I frowned. "I'm assuming you didn't drive."

"No, no, of course not. A friend from Boston came and picked me up."

I smiled, and my eyebrows told her I was surprised. "From Boston?"

"No, Detective, he was visiting for the book launch. He is an old friend."

"This would be one of the friends you had lunch with. May we have a name?"

Her face seemed to dry and harden like plaster. "His name is in your original report. Do you need to trouble him again after all these years?"

"In a case like this, where there is no forensic evidence and there are no witnesses, we need to gather evidence from other sources. Often a simple comment can give us a clue that leads us to an answer. I am sure your friend is totally innocent, but he may know the killer without realizing it. We are trying to catch a murderer, Mrs. Magnusson, not cause you problems."

"Of course." Again the small sigh through her nose and the downcast gaze. "His name is Alornerk, Alornerk Smith. It is in my original statement."

Dehan frowned. "That's a very unusual name, Alornerk."

"It is an Eskimo name. He is from Alaska. He lives and works in Boston. He is a senior lecturer in mathematics. I believe he has changed address since . . ."

Dehan wrote down his new address and phone number. When she was done, I said, "One last thing, could you supply us with a list of your students at Underhill?"

She sagged back in the sofa. "Now?"

I shook my head. "No, but if over the next day or two you could give it some thought and write down everything you can remember about them, that would be helpful."

She gave a nod that was weary. "Yes, very well, Detective Stone, I'll do what I can."

I glanced at Dehan. She shook her head that she had no more questions and we stood. Helena rang a bell, and we stood in awkward silence for a moment. Then Ebba opened the door and led us back down the stairs in a silent procession to the front door. There she smiled her bright smile and said she hoped we would have a lovely day.

The door closed, and we walked without talking back to my old, burgundy Jaguar, where it sat in the mottled spring shade of the green ash.

CHAPTER 2

DEHAN DIDN'T GET IN STRAIGHTAWAY. SHE LEANED HER forearms on the burgundy roof of the car, leaned her chin on her forearms, and drummed her fingers. The dappled shade of the leaves lay across her face.

"In her original statement, she said that Alornerk came to visit and brought a couple of friends with him. She couldn't remember their names, but they were visiting from Europe. She couldn't remember the name of the restaurant either. She had never been there before and Alornerk's friends had chosen it, somewhere in Queens."

I listened to her, then unlocked the car door. "You think she's lying?"

She drummed a bit more, then looked up at the young leaves in the green ash overhead. "It's messy and unlikely enough to be true. It could also be a phony alibi."

I climbed behind the wheel, and she got in the other side. I asked, "What did Alornerk say when they interviewed him?"

She frowned at me and slammed the door. "Read the report sometimes, Stone. That's what it's there for."

"I did, bits. I like to keep it fresh. Besides, I have you to read it for me. I like the way you tell it." The big old engine growled and we pulled away. "What did he say?"

She sighed. "He confirmed her story. The friends had gone back to Europe that evening. It had all been a big shock. He couldn't remember the name of the restaurant either. He would contact the friends and get them to tell him. He never did, and neither of them was ever a suspect, so it wasn't followed up."

I turned into Manhattan Avenue. "You want to go and see Seth Greenway?"

"Of course. Fifteenth floor, 667 Madison Avenue. It's in the file."

"Don't judge me. My father used to judge me. That was what led me into a life of dissolute vice and profligacy, and ultimately self-recrimination and self-loathing. It took years of therapy and analysis to make me the man I am today. But the shadows are never far away. The shadows . . . and the nightmares."

She watched me say all this from behind her aviators, with a small smile on her lips. When I'd finished, she said, "You know all about my family, my history, my childhood, but you never talk about your own past, or your parents."

I shrugged. "Not much to tell. My father was an Austrian sadist with a small moustache and blond eyelashes. He used to pronounce Austria 'orstria.' That always terrified me."

She laughed. I smiled. After a bit I said, "Helena made the point that the killer could be a woman. You think that's significant?"

She shrugged. "I noticed that. I don't know. If she suspected a woman, why not say so? Also, ninety percent of murders are committed by men. So, statistically, it's not likely."

"Statistical probability is a misleading friend, Dehan. Statistically, he is very unlikely to have been murdered in the first place, and yet he was."

"Still, I noticed the comment but personally would not attribute much significance to it."

I made a left and a right onto Central Park West and was

temporarily distracted by the beauty of the grass and the trees in the early spring light. At West 97th I turned into the park. "Would you say she was pedantic—in her speech, I mean?"

She thought about it for a moment. "Yeah, I guess so. She's very precise. You get the feeling she was taught extremely correct English and sticks to the rules."

"I noticed she uses 'shall' in the first person."

She frowned at me. "What?"

"Not many people know that shall is the first person of will: I shall, you will, he will, it will." I glanced at her and went on. "We shall, you will, they will."

"You're kidding."

"She knew that."

"Huh . . ." She frowned again. "Is that important?"

"Well, it makes her question a little more significant, because presumably she knows that in English 'he' is a neutral pronoun as well as a masculine one. That may not be popular in our politically correct age, but she struck me as a woman more concerned with propriety than political correctness. I may be wrong, but I think *she* thinks it was a woman."

She shook her head as we turned out of the park and onto Museum Mile. "One of these days, Stone, you are going to come out with one of these gossamer-thin deductions of yours, and it will be totally wrong."

I snorted. "See? And then you want me to share my thoughts. So that you can erode my ego with cruel, stabbing words, like my mother when she used to make me lie under the floorboards, with the rats."

"You're out of your mind, Stone."

"I must have spring fever."

Five minutes later, I made two lefts onto Madison Avenue and parked outside J. Safra. Dehan opened the door to get out, but I sat drumming the walnut steering wheel and staring at the FedEx van in front of me.

"What?"

"The killer knew where she would be at that time, so he could organize the special delivery."

"Yes."

"He also knew Jack was going for lunch."

"Yup..."

I eyed her face a moment. "So, where did Jack go for lunch?"

"Let's find out."

"Yeah..."

I climbed out and we made our way along the sunlit sidewalk toward 667 Madison Avenue.

We crossed the echoing, toffee-colored marble lobby to the bank of elevators along the far wall, which still evoked Orwell's art deco vision of the future. There, we took a car to the fifteenth floor, in uncomfortable intimacy with a dozen other people, all trying hard to pretend it was normal to be this closely confined with a dozen strangers in a steel box fifteen stories in the air.

The doors slid back, and we exited with relief into the reception of Connors Communication. Here the walls were also marble, but of a pale oxblood hue that was oddly unsettling. A girl who had the kind of charm you learn at customer service school gave us a pretty smile and asked how she might help us.

I showed her my badge.

"I am Detective Stone. This is Detective Dehan. We are investigating a homicide, and we would like to see Mr. Seth Greenway."

She made a call on the internal phone, and two minutes later, a young man in shirtsleeves with hair that looked as though it had been sneezed on came hurrying out of a passage and asked us to please follow him. We did, along a beige-carpeted corridor to a large mahogany door that was guarded by a large mahogany desk. The boy with sticky hair dropped behind the desk and picked up the internal phone.

"Mr. Greenway, the detectives are here..."

He hung up, flicked his eyes at us, and said, "You can go right ahead, through that door."

Dehan raised an eyebrow at him. "Don't get up, junior, I'll get it."

She opened the door and we went in.

Seth Greenway was seated with his back to a floor-to-ceiling, panoramic view of New York City, giving the unsettling feeling that he might at any moment fall backward into empty space. The office was minimalist, with a round table and twelve chairs to one side, hardwood floors with rough-woven mats, and furniture that had that Scandinavian feel which reminded you that comfortable was not the same as cozy.

He looked up from a dozen glossy prints on his desk and stood, smiling at Dehan, holding out his hand as we crossed the room.

"Detectives, forgive me, we are rushed off our feet at the moment with deadlines and the rest of it!" He laughed. "Much like any other time! Please, take a seat."

He glanced at me to include me in the offer to sit and looked back at Dehan with a quizzical frown. "You are investigating a homicide . . ."

I said, "This is a cold case, Mr. Greenway. The murder of the former CEO of this company, Jack Connors."

He flopped back in his big black chair, his mouth sagged a little, and he looked back at Dehan with an oddly reproachful expression. "But that was, oh . . . five years ago."

I answered, even though he was still looking at Dehan. "There is no statute of limitations on homicide, Mr. Greenway. We take a murder committed five years ago just as seriously as one committed this morning."

"Of course!" He glanced at me, spread his hands, and looked back at Dehan. "How can I help?"

She didn't answer. I said, "How well did you know Jack Connors, Mr. Greenway?"

He gave a small shrug. "I probably knew him as well as anybody did. He wasn't really one for sharing his feelings, you know . . ." He laughed at the thought. "He was very much a man's man, a man of action. He was all about getting the job done, pulling in the clients, making the next million. He didn't have time for what he called emotional horseshit." He held up both hands, laughing, and spoke to Dehan again. "I'm not saying I agree. I am just telling you the kind of man he was."

I saw a small frown crease her brow. I smiled. "Was he well liked at work? How did his employees feel about him?"

"Oh . . ." He nodded at me several times, like I had touched on an important point. Then he turned back to Dehan. "Make no mistake. His staff loved him. He was uncompromising, direct to the point of being blunt, sometimes rude, but always fair and a very generous employer. His staff loved him. He never forgot a birthday, if somebody got married the firm would be there to help out, mortgages, insurance, healthcare, deaths in the family . . . You name it, he was there, rolling up his sleeves, getting personally involved to make sure his staff were taken care of."

Dehan gave a small snort. I rubbed my hand over my chin and said, "I'm more interested in what he would have called the emotional horseshit: his personal relationships, friends, enemies, jilted lovers, old girlfriends . . . Who was he close to?" I smiled again. "We are looking for somebody who would want to kill him."

He held my eye a moment, then made a small, helpless gesture with his hands. "Who was he close to? Me and Helena is the simple answer. And I don't think either of us really *knew* him. I am not being awkward, Detective, but the truth is Jack never really got close to anybody. Friends, apart from me, I am not sure he had any. He had acquaintances who were more or less close, with a small *c*, but I am talking about people on his team, who he saw at work. I am not talking about people he socialized with. What little social life he had was all through his wife. You know she is a successful novelist, so often attends events, launches, galas. You know the sort of thing. He would usually accompany her." He took a deep breath and sighed. "Enemies, jilted lovers, old girlfriends. He must have had them, I suppose, he was certainly a man who was attractive to women, but if he did, he never talked about them."

I gazed out at the vast sweep of Manhattan behind him, with the Ed Koch Bridge just visible, spanning the water. I spoke half to myself: "He never socialized..."

"Well," he said quickly, "that would be inaccurate. He *did* socialize, grudgingly, when his wife forced him to."

"What was your impression of their relationship, Mr. Greenway?"

He held my eye and shook his head. "Make no mistake about that, Detective. They adored each other. I have never seen a couple more totally in love."

Dehan spoke for the first time. "How can you know that if he never spoke about emotional horseshit?"

He laughed out loud and his cheeks actually flushed. "He didn't need to talk about it. Whenever you saw them together..." He shook his head, searching for a way to express it. "They were both very reserved, neither of them ever made a public display of affection, but you could just see it in the way they looked at each other, smiled at each other, the small touch of the hand. Everybody agreed, even people who barely knew them. They *adored* each other. And she, I hardly ever see her now, but I know, she never recovered from his death. She used to be bright, lively, fun; but since his death she has just faded away. And her writing! It has become so dark!"

I gave a small sigh and rubbed my chin again. The picture I was getting, both from Helena and from Greenway, was almost absurdly detailed and yet told me nothing about the man. I went for the question that had been playing on my mind.

"You say he never socialized unless it was with his wife. So, where did he go for lunch that Thursday at one p.m.?"

For a moment he reminded me vaguely of a goldfish, staring at me with round eyes, his mouth working on unformed words which never made it past his larynx. Dehan said, "Presumably he had a secretary, and a diary."

He scratched his eyebrow and stammered, "Long, long . . . um . . . long since departed, I'm afraid . . ."

"You mentioned a team."

"As I say, that was about five years ago. There was Jean Reynolds, Angie Byrne, Peter Heseltine . . . Those are the names that come to mind. Angie was the graphic designer, Jean and Peter came from backgrounds in CG, animation, special effects, that kind of thing. They all had creative input."

"They still with the company?"

"Oh, yes, they are still with us, we value . . ."

"Could we talk to them?"

He gave a laugh that was more stress than humor. "They are actually engaged in a presentation right now that is worth several million dollars to the company. Let me arrange it and tomorrow, the day after at the very latest, you can sit down with them and have their full attention."

I smiled like someone who wants to be cooperative. "We'd appreciate that."

Dehan scratched the tip of her nose and asked, "Mr. Greenway, who benefited from Jack Connors' death?"

He opened his mouth, his eyebrows moved in various ways, and he blinked several times.

"Ah . . . *Nobody* benefited from Jack's death. Helena inherited a lot of money and property that was, in effect, *already hers*! She inherited controlling shares in this company, *which she did not want*, because she had zero interest in it; and she ended up selling *me* a bundle of shares. So there was no real material benefit there, but she *did* lose a man whom she was very much in love with.

"You are probably thinking that I benefited by becoming CEO, but you're wrong. Jack was planning to take early retirement anyway, and we had already discussed how he was going to transfer the reins of the company to me, and with them a bundle of shares. As it turned out, I had to buy those shares from Helena, so I actually lost money, and also the support and guidance of a businessman who was frankly brilliant. I miss him every day as a guide and a mentor. Emotional horseshit no doubt, but true nonetheless."

I stared at him a moment, chewing my lip and thinking that he sounded sincere. After a moment he spread his hands and said, "Detectives, forgive me for being blunt, but we are up against tight deadlines, and I don't see that I can be much more help to you."

I nodded slowly a few times. Dehan turned to look at me. I said, "There is just one last question, Mr. Greenway. Who was he having the affair with?"

He closed his eyes and sighed heavily. "I don't know, Detective Stone. I believe he strayed a few times over the years. He never talked about it, but there were telltale signs . . ." He gestured at me. "As you noted, going out for lunch, which was totally uncharacteristic, not collecting his wife from college to take her to the book launch. It was atypical behavior and strongly suggestive of an affair. But I cannot swear to the fact, nor do I know who he was involved with."

Dehan narrowed her eyes at him. "Did she know?"

"Helena?" He hesitated. "She is a highly intelligent woman, very deep and very intuitive. I would be very surprised if she didn't know, but I suspect they both accepted it. For him it was a biological need, and she just accepted that that was the kind of man he was."

Dehan raised an eyebrow. "A man's man."

Greenway shook his head. "Don't attack me, Detective. I don't condone what he did. I am just telling you how I *think* they dealt with it. We never discussed it, and I have no idea what went on in their private lives."

There was a tap at the door and it opened. I turned to look. It was a small man in a suit. He was perhaps in his midthirties with a face that was not unpleasant, but not particularly pleasant either. The only way to describe him was to say that he was nondescript. He stopped dead when he saw us and said, "Oh, I'm sorry . . ."

Seth groaned and managed to turn it into a sigh. "Peter, come in, close the door. These are Detectives Dehan and Stone. They are investigating Jack's murder, five years ago."

His eyes were round, with small lashes. He approached, staring from Dehan to me and back again. He said, "Oh . . ." He looked past us then, at Seth, and said, "We finished the presentation. It went really well. The girls and I have been on our feet for thirty-six hours, we were going to go home if that's okay . . ."

"Of course . . ."

I stood. "Mr. Greenway, thank you for your help. Peter . . ." I turned to him. "We'll walk you down. We have a couple of questions we'd like to ask you. It won't take more than a couple of minutes."

CHAPTER 3

We traveled down in the elevator with Peter and Angie Byrne. Dehan smiled at them and said, "You carpooling? Got far to go?"

Angie, who had merino wool instead of hair, rolled her eyes and said, "I wish! No! It's public transport for us, ay, Peter?"

Peter's eyes were firmly on the floor. "I'm afraid so."

"I'm sharing an apartment on 116th. But poor Peter is all the way over in the Bronx."

"We're going that way, we'll give you a ride. Right, Stone?"

"Sure, I'm right outside. So you guys were both in Jack's team?"

Angie nodded her shaggy head. "Are you investigating his murder? But that was like, what . . . ?" She looked at Peter.

He said, "October seventh, 2014. Four and a half years ago."

"Is that like a cold case?"

I nodded. "How well did you know him?"

She looked at Peter when she answered. "He wasn't easy to know. He was all about the work. He didn't encourage personal conversation . . ."

Peter snorted. "He was loud, rude, bombastic. Everybody here reveres his memory because he was murdered, but the truth is, he was a first-class jerk."

Dehan gave a short laugh. "That's refreshing. It's what I've been picking up all day but nobody has come out and said it till now. Is that a personal grudge?"

He echoed her laugh but shook his head. "Not at all. He was a great employer, and CC is a great place to work, but he was a jerk and an ego freak."

The doors slid back, and we made our way out to the sidewalk. As we approached the car, Peter said, "Jaguars are very unreliable. Especially the older models."

I unlocked the door. "You ever own a Jaguar?"

His glance was resentful. "No."

We all climbed in, the cat growled, and we pulled out into the stream of traffic. I jumped right in. "So it was common knowledge that Jack was having an affair?"

In the mirror I saw them glance at each other. Angie started to say, "I wouldn't say common knowledge . . ."

But Peter cut in. "Yes."

"No, Peter . . ."

"Come on, Angie! He used to talk to her on the phone, right there in front of us!"

Dehan glanced over her shoulder at them. "How can you be sure?"

Peter's voice took an almost hectoring tone. "Because, even though Jack liked to put it about that he was a private, reserved kind of guy, in *fact* he also liked it to be known that he *put it about* in a different way! So we'd be having a meeting to discuss a campaign or a contract or whatever, and he would receive a call, and . . ."

Angie sighed loudly. "Peter! You don't *know* . . ."

"No, listen. Let me ask you something. If you were having an illicit affair, and you were in a meeting, and you *really*—I mean *truthfully* didn't want anybody to know you were having an affair, how would you deal with the call?" He paused, and nobody answered, so he went on, putting his thumb and baby finger to his ear and mouth. "'Hello . . . no, I'm afraid this is not a good time. Perhaps you could call back at seven. Thank you, goodbye.' Or would you stand up, walk away from the table, and in a loud stage whisper say, '*Penelope! I have told you a thousand times not to call me at work! . . . Yes, I love you too, baby . . . I miss you too . . . Look, I'm in the middle of a meeting, I'll call you later.*'"

It was like the butler had just farted while serving the queen her sherry. The silence was like a physical object in the car. I glanced at Angie in the mirror. "Would you agree with that, Angie? Was it like that?"

She sighed again. "Yeah, it was pretty much like that. I mean, he was a pain in the ass, but he was also brilliant at what he did, and a great boss."

Peter rolled his eyes. "The police are not here to investigate whether he was a great boss or not, Angie . . ."

She cut across him. "And also there is the impact on Helena. Have you guys met Helena yet? She is such a sweet, kind, lovely woman. Everybody loves her, and what she does for underprivileged people? Man! You know her salary for teaching creative writing goes straight to charity?"

I asked her, "What impact would it have on her?"

"She was really in love with Jack. Bad enough that he was murdered like that—and being sent his head in a *box*? Man, that is *harsh*! But to know that he was cheating on her as well?"

We had come to East 116th and I pulled in opposite her apartment. Angie went to get out, but Dehan turned in her seat to look at her.

"Angie? That is a sweet sentiment, but it is not a good reason to lie to the cops or suppress evidence. That's a very serious offense. Do you understand that?" Her cheeks colored. Dehan went on. "A man was murdered, and you would have the killer go free so as not to upset the wife? I don't think you thought that one through, did you?"

"No, I guess not . . . I'm sorry . . . I'd better go."

She got out, and we watched her hurry across the road. I did a U, and we continued on our way to the Bronx. Peter was in the mood to talk.

"You know? We get regular seminars in NLP, neurolinguistic programming? It's kind of gone out of fashion now, but Jack was a big advocate, and Seth is too. And one of the main points about NLP is that some people think mainly in pictures, some people think mainly in words and sounds, and some people think with their feelings. That's Angie. Like you said, Detective Dehan, they don't follow through and analyze the consequences and implications of that first feeling. They just allow the feeling to kind of rule them. It was crazy, Jack was killed and there was like an automatic conspiracy of silence to protect Helena."

I frowned at him in the mirror. "You telling me that the whole staff lied to the original investigators?"

He shook his head. "No, nothing so black and white as that. Jack never came out and said, 'I am having an affair,' therefore none of us *knew* that he was having an affair, and as they were both quite obviously very fond of each other, the collective conclusion was that he was *not* having an affair. So nobody lied, but nobody told the whole truth either."

Dehan said, "So, Penelope? Was that her name?"

"Yep, Penelope Peach."

Dehan grinned and looked over her shoulder again. "Penelope Peach? Are you kidding?"

"No, that's her name. It's a hard name to forget. I heard him dictating her name and address over the phone. He was having something delivered to her. I don't know what. I can't remember the address, but it was on the Upper West Side, not far from his own house."

I studied him a moment in the rearview. "You didn't like him much, did you?"

"Not really. I didn't dislike him much either. I thought he was a narcissistic egomaniac, and it kind of annoyed me that everybody bought into his 'firm-but-fair' great guy act." He gave a small shrug. "He was living proof that his system worked. He was a crass, vulgar oaf, but he *told* everybody he was an amazing guy, and they all believed him."

Dehan gave a single nod and pulled down the corners of her mouth. "Is that what persuasion engineering is?"

"It's a little more complex than that, but in essence, yes. It's based on the idea that communication is *always* what the other person understands. If in my language 'I love you' means 'I hate you,' and I say to you, 'Detective Dehan, I love you,' what I have communicated is the opposite of what I actually intended to communicate. My intention plays no part in the communication. Communication is what you understand, not what I intend."

I gave a small grunt. "That's pretty obvious, isn't it?"

"On the surface, perhaps. But then consider that each individual has his own language. Ninety-three percent of all communication is nonverbal. We communicate in hugely complex ways: tone, expression, twitches, gestures, body language—all of which flow from our unconscious urges, needs, fears, and appetites; and all of that complex bundle is our own, personal language. So a skilled communicator takes the trouble to learn the language of the person he wants to communicate to, and tells them what they want them to hear, see, and feel, in *their own language*. Jack was a passed master at that."

"But you didn't buy into it?"

He laughed. "Jack never thought I was important enough to learn my language. Consequently, I saw through him, and he didn't even see me."

"How about Helena?"

We were on the bridge, and I saw him look out of the window at the wide expanse of water. "I think it suited them both to present this image of a united couple deeply in love with each other. I think they really were fond, but I also suspect they had stopped being in love a long time ago."

Dehan had turned and wedged her back against the door so she could see him. "How well did you know her?"

I saw him smile out at the water. Then he turned to face her. "Maybe I could start my own business teaching NLP to the NYPD. Then you might start asking more subtle questions. I didn't know her very well at all. She would sometimes come into the office, charm everyone, be superbly, elegantly European, and then leave. I am not a brilliant observer, there are people at work who are real masters. They call it calibration. They will actually detect changes in your skin texture and breathing pattern while they speak to you. But I'm not that good."

"I read somewhere that NLP is basically a form of hypnosis."

"Not basically, that is exactly what it is. And not *a* form, but many forms. NLP is a range of highly sophisticated techniques for putting people into trance and manipulating their unconscious while they're there."

We were quiet for a while as we drove along the Bruckner Expressway, headed east. As I moved off, onto the boulevard to take White Plains north, he said, "I did try to talk to Detective Langstrum, during the original investigation, but he didn't seem very interested. I guess because everybody else was giving him the official version."

We dropped him outside his house on St. Lawrence Avenue and watched him push through the gate, unlock the white door, and go inside. When he was gone from view, I pulled out and we made our way back toward Story Avenue and the station. Neither of us spoke until I had parked the car and killed the engine. Then I looked at Dehan and said, "I am trying to work out what happened just there."

She nodded. "Me too. Roast beef sandwiches and coffee might help. You go get 'em, big guy, I'll search for Penelope Peach. Like the man said, there can't be many of them."

"Sounds like a plan."

When I got back from the deli and put the brown paper bag on the desk, Dehan was on the phone, sounding sweet and friendly.

"Oh, she's not there right now? But you think she'll be back next Monday? With friends . . . I bet she has! Well, how about you, honey? You sound like you are just *gorgeous*! We have a *superb range* . . . Well what are you *laughin' at*? Nobody ever told you you sound beautiful? Well, I just don't *believe* that!" She reached over and took a beef sandwich from the bag, checked it for pickles, and gave me the thumbs-up. "Okay, honey, well, I'll call back Monday, but you think about what I told you. Bye now!"

She hung up and bit into the sandwich. I said, "I think you derive a perverse pleasure from these personae you adopt."

"Personae?"

"I gather she is visiting friends for the weekend."

She spoke with her mouth full. "Dere a' chew Phenelophe Peash im Mew Ork shtate." She swallowed. "Only one in New York City. Flat A, tenth floor, 464 Riverside Drive. She's in the right class for him to have noticed she existed and engineered some persuasion."

I sat, took a bite of my own sandwich, and asked, "Have we got a picture?"

"Gorgeous. She's an actress, so she has a small presence online."

My phone pinged, and when I checked, she had sent me a picture of a partly clothed woman of prominent charms. I shrugged. "Not my type. Too . . ." I shook my head. "Too too."

"Yeah? I think you're in a minority."

"You got a cell?"

She nodded. "And her GPS is switched on." She pointed at her screen. "She's in Madison, Connecticut. She's at a big house on Lantern Hill Road."

"Dystopia is alive and well."

"You want to call ahead or be all dystopian and just turn up? 'Vee know vere you are! Vee can finet you anyvere unt make you obey!'"

"That sounds like fun, but I think we'll call and see if she's willing to talk to us. If she's not, we can try some persuasion engi-

BLOOD INTO WINE | 209

neering." She tossed me a piece of paper with a number on it. "Something tells me she'll be more responsive to a man."

"You're a cynic, Dehan. I bet she's a really nice person."

I dialed and waited while it rang. After a moment, it stopped, and a voice like the chiming of tiny silver bells said, "Hel-lo-hoo! Penny Peach speaking!"

I inserted a fatherly smile into my voice, avoided eye contact with Dehan, and said, "Ah, Miss Peach, this is Detective John Stone of the NYPD."

"Oh, Lord." A small giggle. "What have I done?"

I laughed. "Nothing that I am aware of, Miss Peach. I head up the cold-cases unit here at the Forty-Third Precinct in the Bronx, and we were hoping to ask you some questions about an old case we are investigating."

There was a long silence. I was about to ask if she was still there when she said, "What case, Detective?"

The acoustics and the sound quality had changed, and I gathered she had moved away to a more private spot.

"This would have been about four and a half years ago . . ."

I left the words hanging, curious about how she would respond. Her response was a half-hearted laugh and, "You're teasing me."

"Do you know what case I am referring to, Miss Peach?"

"I'm not sure."

"If you were sure, what would it be?"

"Was it a homicide?"

"This is not a guessing game, Miss Peach."

"Jack . . . ?"

"Would you be willing to talk to us this afternoon? We believe you might have information that could be very helpful in our investigation. As I am sure you can appreciate, it is vitally important that we eliminate you from our inquiry."

"Eliminate *me*? Am I a *suspect*?"

"Not right now, and the best way to avoid becoming one is to cooperate fully with us. We will be discreet, Miss Peach, and if your relationship with him is not relevant to the murder, it need never become public knowledge."

I heard a small sigh. "Yes, all right, when will you be here?"

"In about two hours."

"Okay, I'll see you in two hours at Cristy's, on Wharf Road. And, Detective, please do be discreet. I am here with my fiancé at his senior partner's house. There is a lot riding on this visit."

I glanced at Dehan and smiled. "I'm John, my partner is Carmen, we're just passing through and we thought we'd look you up. Let's make it the Madison Beach Hotel, we'll be staying over till the morning."

". . . Thank you. That's very . . . sensitive of you. Carmen is a lucky woman."

"See you in a couple of hours."

I hung up. "Well, Carmen, how do you fancy dinner at the Madison Beach Hotel?"

"Do they do bison steak?"

"No, but they do prime fourteen-ounce, twenty-one-day aged New York strip, roasted garlic smashed potato, grilled asparagus, applewood smoked bacon butter, and crispy leeks."

"Sold to the girl with the appetite. Let's go talk to daddy's latest fan."

We stood, and I saw Mo, large and pale with his shirt untucked, staring at us from the next desk across the aisle. He shook his head. "Do you two know how nauseating you are?"

Dehan pulled on her jacket and grinned. "What are you having for dinner, Mo?"

"Get lost."

"Who knows? We might, tramping barefoot along Madison Beach; see where our wandering footsteps take us."

"Yeah," he growled at the papers on his desk. "Here's hoping."

We left.

Scan the QR code below to purchase JACK IN THE BOX.
Or go to: righthouse.com/jack-in-the-box